IN NEED OF HANGING

Thad Palmer is hunting Vince Long — on a trail littered with raped, beaten women and cold-blooded killings. Now, led into the valley where his own sweetheart awaits his return, he knows that she's in danger from Long, but his heart races at the prospect of being with Coralee. But as Thad reaches the budding settlement, he is unaware of the rifle barrel trained on him. Can Thad save himself and the life of the ones he holds dear?

BILLY HALL

IN NEED OF HANGING

Complete and Unabridged

LINFORD
Leicester

First published in Great Britain in 2011 by
Robert Hale Limited
London

First Linford Edition
published 2013
by arrangement with
Robert Hale Limited
London

British Library CIP Data

Hall, Billy.
   In need of hanging.- -
   (Linford western library)
   1. Western stories.
   2. Large type books.
   I. Title II. Series
   823.9'2–dc23

ISBN 978–1–4448–1418–7

Published by
F. A. Thorpe (Publishing)
Anstey, Leicestershire

Set by Words & Graphics Ltd.
Anstey, Leicestershire
Printed and bound in Great Britain by
T. J. International Ltd., Padstow, Cornwall
This book is printed on acid-free paper

1

Red dawn tinged the earth with crimson blush. It seemed only right. The earth should flush with shame. Even the earth herself should feel the disgrace of the things done upon her in the night.

It was not the dawn Vince Long had expected. It should have dawned gray and dreary, like his mood. Stormy, perhaps, with remnants of red-hot anger still streaking the skies. Instead it was this bright rosy blush of shame that colored the world as far as he could see.

He rode his horse at a swift trot. Occasionally he cast a glance over his shoulder. He kept to the low ground, avoiding exposing himself as much as possible.

It wasn't how he had envisioned this day. This was the day he had expected to ride tall and proudly. He had expected to exult in finally being the man he had so long dreamed of becoming.

He tried to remember her name. What was it, she had told him? He couldn't remember. He should at least have been able to remember that. She had been his first.

He had anticipated it all so carefully. He had listened carefully to every ribald bunkhouse story told in his presence. He had mentally rehearsed every word, every action, everything he planned to say and do. He had even practiced his responses to what he knew she would do and say.

It had started feeling wrong right away in the saloon. He had visited the barber, for a haircut, a shave, a bath. His clothes were brand-new and clean. He had chewed a couple sage leaves he had picked on his way to town, to make even his breath pleasant. He had done everything those stories had mentioned to prepare for this experience.

Now that he was here, he began to

have misgivings. None of the working girls in the saloon was as pretty as his fantasies had imagined. They all looked tired, hard, bored even. The expression, 'rode hard and put up wet', echoed unexpectedly in his mind.

A couple drinks helped that a lot, though. His interest began to grow again. One of the girls in particular looked a lot better when she smiled at him.

He offered to buy her a drink, which she readily accepted. He knew her drink was probably tea, and that she got a cut of the drinks cowboys bought for her. He'd heard that in the bunkhouse too. He didn't really care. That was part of the game, he knew, and he had come to play that game.

After a few minutes of small talk, he used his well-practiced invitation to go upstairs with him. She responded just as he knew she would. As soon as they were inside the small room, she mentioned the price. In advance, of course. He'd known that was exactly how it would be. He'd listened to the bunkhouse stories carefully. He paid her his two dollars. She put it away. But then she just unceremoniously told him to drop his trousers. Just like that.

'Drop your britches, cowboy.'

That wasn't the way it was supposed to be. It was supposed to be at least a little bit romantic, he thought. They were supposed to hug and kiss or something. He'd get fresh, and she'd giggle and encourage him. Then he'd begin to unbutton her bodice. He was sure that was the way it was supposed to work. But she didn't even offer that.

He did as he was told, knowing he was blushing furiously. He hoped she didn't look up at his face and notice. She didn't. She just took hold of him, washed him with some funny-smelling water like she was washing dishes or something.

It felt good, though, the way she stroked him as she washed. He had to admit that. It did feel good.

But then she just lay down on the bed, hiked up her dress, and said, 'OK.

Mount up, cowboy. Let's see what you've got.'

She made it seem just like branding a calf. Or topping off a raw bronc. Just get it done. It was as if she were saying, 'Get your job over with, so I can go back downstairs.'

For one brief moment he considered walking out. Even as the thought crossed his mind, he knew he wouldn't. He had put in a lot of thought and preparation for this moment. He had carefully worked up enough courage to make the attempt. And he was young. He was determined. He was eager. Too eager. It was over before he even got started.

That was it? That was all there was to it? Disappointment and embarrassment flooded through him. He got to his feet and hastily pulled his pants back on.

Then she laughed at him. She looked at him, and just laughed. 'Don't worry about it, little boy,' she had said. 'It's always like that the first time. You'll grow up.'

She didn't look at all pretty any more. She looked old and used. Hard lines around her mouth reflected the flat stare of her eyes. The harsh laugh and mocking smile roused a virulent anger that surged instantly and violently within him. She called him 'little boy'. He suddenly hated her more than he could ever remember hating another human being.

He didn't remember even reaching for the large knife that was always in its sheath at his belt. He didn't remember pulling it from its leather keeper. It was just there, in his hand, tightly enough gripped that his knuckles were white. His disappointment and anger and hatred rose to levels beyond his waning control.

As if possessed of a mind of its own, the knife slid between her ribs smoothly, effortlessly. Clear to the hilt. It even seemed to be its own idea to move its point sideways, so the end sliced a path within her chest. It slid back out again, before she even realized how much her mocking laughter had infuriated him. Shock instantly erased the hardness of her face. She turned ashen. Her hard, flat eyes suddenly radiated pain and terror. She opened her mouth and tried to speak. No words came out.

Strangely, no blood followed the knife as it left the wound. The wound clamped closed, almost as if trying in vain to hold the life within its walls of flesh.

Everything seemed to happen with maddening slowness. Entranced, he watched the changing expressions cross her face. He saw her sag with sudden weakness, sliding off the edge of the mattress.

He looked at her feet as they slid strangely forward on the bare wooden boards. He watched her sit down with a thud on the floor. She leaned back against the bed. Her eyes glazed over. All color washed from her face, leaving her as white as the dingy, spotted sheet. Her head lolled backward onto the thin mattress. Both hands flopped down on the floor, palms up.

Her mouth sagged open. In death she was even uglier than when she was alive, he thought.

Moving as if in a daze, he wiped the knife's blade clean on the sheet and replaced it in its sheath. He picked up his hat. He walked woodenly out of the door, down the stairs. He kept his eyes fixed on the outside door, ignoring everyone and everything else. He marched resolutely through the saloon and into the street. Nobody paid him any least attention.

He untied his horse from the hitch rail and mounted. He braced himself for the shout of alarm, the clamor of pursuit, maybe even gunfire behind him. There was nothing. The town seemed as peaceful as a sleeping nursery. He rode out of town at a swift trot.

He was miles away now, heading he knew not where. Everything he owned was rolled up in his bedroll, tied behind the saddle, and in the saddlebags. He was between jobs anyway. It didn't matter where he went. There were always ranches looking for hands. And he was a good cow hand. Better with horses, even. Every ranch needed a top-notch wrangler.

The embarrassed rose blush of the dawn's shame had faded quickly. The sun was up now. Sunshine always helps. Everything began to seem better. Maybe it wasn't the end of the world, after all. It was her fault anyway. Next time he'd find a better woman, and it would be different. Maybe he'd find a woman who wasn't a whore. Other women could be persuaded, bunkhouse talk said.

One old cowboy told endless stories about a church choir leader he'd been with often, until she had gotten pregnant. He boasted that he would probably have married her, but she had died in childbirth. Maybe he could find a woman like that. He'd find a woman who actually wanted him, next time. One who didn't laugh at him, at least. Next time.

2

'Are you Thad Palmer?'

Thad's hand dropped instantly to the butt of his gun. 'I 'spect I must be. That's what folks call me, anyway.'

'You're a gunfighter, aren't you?'

Thadeus Palmer studied the rancher standing before him. The man stood with his legs slightly spread. His shoulders were hunched just a couple inches above a comfortable position. His mouth was set in a look of grim determination. His eyes reflected fear, Thad thought. He was sure that if he said 'boo', real loud, the man would turn and run. It obviously took every ounce of the man's courage to stand his ground.

'That ain't usually a real healthy question to ask a man,' he replied softly.

Something, maybe a deeper measure of fear, flashed in the rancher's eyes. It was instantly replaced by a look of grim determination. 'I know that,' he said simply. 'I just gotta know. One of my neighbors pointed you out to me. He said you was the fastest gunfighter he'd ever seen.'

'What do you want with a gun-fighter?'

'I wanta hire you.'

'To do what?'

The man sighed as if struggling to breathe beneath some intolerable weight. 'That'll take a bit of explainin'. If you're willin' to listen, I'll buy you a drink and we'll talk.'

Thad studied the man a long moment. He was running low on cash money. He had turned down half a dozen offers of work, because he was choosy. Too choosy, for a gunfighter.

He would be happy to hire on as a working cowboy. That was the life he really wanted. Better even, would be a ranch of his own. His reputation and his immediately obvious skill with a gun made that almost impossible.

Even so, he wasn't willing to hire his gun to anything or anyone he considered wrong. There were always plenty of jobs like that available. The shady and outright crooked people always seemed to have a ready reserve of available cash to offer whomever they chose to hire. Honest folks in a bind always had greater need, but usually little or no cash. And a man had to live.

To make it worse, the jobs a gunfighter was hired for didn't usually last too long, as a rule. Either you lost and died, or you succeeded, and worked yourself out of a job. Either way, you were either unemployed or dead in short order.

'I'll listen,' he said finally.

The rancher spun on his heel and headed for the saloon, leaving Thad to follow. Inside, he tossed some money on the bar, got a bottle and a couple more or less clean glasses. He walked to a table at the opposite end of the room. He started to sit, then changed his mind. He moved to a seat with his back to the room.

'Thanks,' Thad said, grateful that the man had deliberately left him the seat with its back to the wall.

The rancher didn't answer. He poured a drink into each glass and slid one across the table to Thad. Each took a moment to sip the harsh liquid, then savor the glow as it passed down their throats, then began to spread its glow outward from their stomachs.

'Odd how somethin' that's sure to ruin you can feel so good goin' down,' Thad mused.

The pained look that crossed the rancher's face made him immediately regret the comment. He moved to change the subject immediately. 'So, who are you, and why do you wanta hire a gunfighter?'

The weathered rancher took a deep breath. 'My name's Chaps Turner. Me and the missus run the Rockin' C T ranch. It's about thirty miles up north o' here.'

'I've heard of it,' Thad acknowledged.

'You have?'

'Yeah. I played a little poker a while back with a kid who works for you. Or did, anyway. Guy by the name of Billy Dellenbach, if I remember right.'

Chaps nodded his head. 'Billy's been with me three or four years. Good cowboy. Comes to town every three or four months and blows all the wages he's got comin'. I usually know about when to come to town to get him. By the time I get here, he's usually got his saddle and his rifle and his pocket watch pawned. I bail 'im out and take 'im back home, and he's good for another three or four months.'

'Typical cowboy.'

'Seems that way. Most of 'em grow up eventually, though. At least if they find a good woman and settle down. They ain't that much different than I was at that age.'

'The ones that live long enough,' Thad guardedly agreed.

'Yeah, there's a lot that don't,' Chaps agreed.

'So you're Chaps Turner and you run the Rocking C T. Why do you need a gunfighter?'

The look Thad had noticed immediately when they met now returned to Chaps's eyes. His shoulders hunched up again. Thad realized suddenly it wasn't fear he saw in the man at all. It was some deep, long-term sadness that weighed like a sodden pall on him.

It was obvious that whatever it was had nearly broken the man.

'Well, it started several years ago,' Chaps said. He paused and sipped the whiskey in his glass. 'Me and the missus got . . . we had . . . three kids. The boys was a bit wild and wooly, but good boys. Sorta like Billy, that you met. He puts me in mind of my boys. Martin and Tuffy grew up, settled down, got married. They both got places close to mine.'

'That's gotta make you proud.'

'Yeah, it helps. The third kid was a

girl. Lucy. Lucille Belle Turner. Pretty girl. Tomboy, like most ranch girls. The boys tagged her 'Lucifer' when they wanted to torment her. She always managed to get even. She could ride and rope and shoot and flank down a calf every bit as good as the boys. Then she went and turned into a young woman.'

'That seems to happen.'

Chaps ignored the comment. 'We had a string o' lovestruck cowboys filin' through the yard that'd reach pertneart to Laramie. A fight'd bust out about once a week betwixt 'em. I just prayed we'd all last long enough she'd pick one of 'em and get married and stop bustin' hearts.'

'Waitin' for the right one, huh?'

'Seemed so. Then she found him. Or thought she did. And he seemed like a winner. Even had the name for it. His name was Winston Schultz. Folks called him Win. Good lookin' young fella. Hell on high wheels in a fight. Good with stock. Anyway, they got married.'

'But no 'happily ever after', I take it.'

'No, not hardly. They wasn't much more'n past the honeymoon when we started noticin' bruises here an' there on Lucy. If we asked about 'em, she'd just say somethin' about bein' clumsy, or somethin' fallin' over on 'er. Then she got pregnant. We was plumb happy. She was too, for quite a while.'

He paused, staring into space for quite a while. Thad held his silence, letting the man gather his thoughts.

Chaps took another sip of his whiskey. 'Well, to make a long story short, she come home one day all beat to heck. Bawlin' her head off. Looked like she'd tangled with a grizzly bear. When she got the story out, she told us Win had got mad at her, beat her up, kicked her in the belly, made her lose the baby. Then the next day he started in on her again. She just grabbed his gun and shot 'im.'

'Good for her.'

'Yeah. Danged shame she didn't do it on her weddin' night.'

17

'Would've saved a lot of trouble.'

'Yeah, well, life don't seem to work that way. Nothin' ever works out the way you figger it's gonna.'

He seemed lost in thought for two or three minutes. His voice was soft, almost pensive, when he spoke again. 'Me and the missus, we fought droughts and blizzards, fought our way through years that was too wet and years that was too dry. We fought Indians and rustlers and crooked neighbors. We always figured as long as we stood together, we could fight just about anything.'

He paused again, then continued. 'There's some things you just can't fight though. Lucy, she took to havin' longer and longer periods of melancholy. Wouldn't get outa bed for a week at a time, sometimes. Lay there an' wet the bed sometimes, instead o' gettin' up to walk to the outhouse. Then she'd snap out of it, and seem to do pretty good.

'Then she run off with another

good-lookin' cowboy. She came back a couple months later, and asked, could she come home?'

'Hard to say no.'

'We couldn't say no.'

He took a deep, ragged breath and continued. 'Somewhere along there she started drinkin'. Not just once in a while. Regular, like.'

'Deadened the pain some, probably.'

'I 'spect. Then she run off with a gamblin' man she met in town. I figured she probably met him in the saloon, but I didn't never tell the missus that. I didn't want her to know Lucy'd sunk low enough to be spendin' time in a saloon.'

'That had to hurt.'

'That made me hurt worse than I ever thought anything could make me hurt. Anyway, I'm way too long to make this story short, but the fact is, she ended up on the line.'

'In the saloon?'

'Yeah. One saloon or another. It didn't seem to matter what one. After

19

while, she stopped hidin' the fact that she was a whore. She stayed in contact with us. She'd come home once in a while for a day or two. Usually when she was comin' down off of a long drunk. We put up with it. We kept the door open for her. We just kept hopin' and prayin' that one day she'd get over it, straighten up her life, and amount to somethin'.'

'Where there's life there's hope.'

'That's what we always figured. Well, it didn't happen. It might've. I'll always think it would've, eventually. She didn't live long enough.'

'She died?'

'She got killed, over in Lone Tree.'

'How?'

'One of her . . . customers . . . stabbed her to death.'

'Really? Why?'

Chaps picked up his glass and drained it. He stared into the bottom of the empty container, fighting for control. He shook his head. 'Don't know for sure. I 'spect, knowin' Lucy, she said somethin' that set 'im off.'

'Do you know who did it?'

He nodded. 'The bartender knowed who she'd gone upstairs with. Cowboy. Young fella by the name o' Vince Long. He'd been working for the J-Cross for quite a while.

'Do you know why he did it?'

'Not for sure. I got an idea. The boys I talked to out there told me they figured he hadn't never been with a woman before. Lucy, she always had a sharp tongue, even as a kid. That's one reason her brothers teased her by callin' her 'Lucifer'. Then, after she changed an' all, she had a tongue that'd blister the paint off'n a new red wagon. She could say things that'd make a soldier blush in shame. I'm guessin' . . . and this is just a guess, mind you. Nobody knows for sure. But I'm guessin', what with bein' the boy's first time an' all, he likely embarrassed himself some. Bein' Lucy, she woulda said somethin' that wasn't exactly kindly.

He couldn't take it, so he took it out on her. That's what I'm guessin'.'

Thad mulled it over in his mind as Chaps poured himself another drink. 'That would make sense,' he said at last. 'But it doesn't tell me why you want to hire a gunfighter.'

Chaps fought for control for a long moment again. Slowly, anger built up in him and crowded out the heaviness of his unbearable grief. 'I know what Lucy was, what she'd become. I know what kind of mouth she had on her. But she was still a woman. She was still my daughter.'

He paused again, clearly fighting to control his emotions. His voice quivered as he said, 'Even a whore don't never stop bein' her daddy's little girl. I want the man that murdered my little girl brung to justice. I want him shot or hung. I want him caught.'

'He skipped the country?'

'Oh, yeah. He lit out afore anyone even knowed Lucy was dead.'

'Why doesn't the law go after him?'

Chaps snorted. 'What law? The town marshal ran outa jurisdiction as soon as Long was outa town. The US marshals have more important things to do than spend a lot o' time trackin' down someone that didn't do nothin' worse than killin' a whore. Naw, there ain't a lawman in the country that's gonna waste a day of his precious time on it.'

'So that's what you want me to do?'

'That's what I want you to do. Tell me what kinda wages you get. I'll pay you as much at a time as you want. I want you to get on his trail and keep on it till you find him.'

'It could take a while.'

'I don't care how long it takes. He's needin' hangin', and I sure don't wanta deprive him of it.'

'How do you know I won't just take your money and ride on?'

'I don't. But the ones I asked tell me you're straight. You just give me your word. That's all I've ever asked of any man.'

Thad considered it a long moment.

Whatever the provocation, anyone who murdered a woman needed hanging. What the woman was didn't really matter. What she had done or said didn't either. That was just the way it was. Besides, he needed a job. He could do worse.

'Well, I guess you just hired yourself a gunfighter.'

3

It looked peaceful enough. Too peaceful. There should be at least a
buckboard or two tied up in front of the
general store. Its sign boasted 'food-
stuffs, dry goods, and hardware.' That
just about covered the necessities for
most ranches. That nobody was in town
for supplies seemed odd.

Thad Palmer sat his horse at the end
of the town's lone business street,
frowning. That something ominous
waited for him here seemed obvious to
his carefully honed senses. He had
survived this long by never ignoring
those instincts. What it was that
triggered those instincts was not immediately apparent.

He was tired, dusty, out of sorts. The
last thing he wanted was anything that
would interfere with his having a room
at the hotel, a halfway decent bed, a hot

meal, a bath, and a good night's sleep.

He had been two weeks on the trail of the man he was hired to find. Vince Long had left Lone Tree in a big hurry. Nobody was sure even what direction he had gone. It had taken a full week of circling, asking questions, quizzing cowboys, ranchers, sheep-herders, drifters, before he had a firm fix on the direction of the young man's travel.

That direction would make this town a definite possibility. His presence here wouldn't explain the absence of activity in the town, though.

He shrugged and nudged his horse forward, past the crooked sign with faded paint boasting, 'Paradise Corner'.

He didn't have to nudge his horse hard, or use his spurs. He and this horse had traveled enough miles together they virtually read each other's mind. Tom knew his rider well.

Tom was a good-sized gelding. Fifteen hands. Mottled color. Thick chested. He could keep going for longer stretches than any horse Thad had ever seen.

Tom did like to buck a little of a morning. Not hard bucking. Just crow-hopping enough to work out the night's kinks. Each day, the first time Thad mounted him, he'd buck that way for a few jumps, then he was ready for a day's ride.

Even in that, he seemed to read Thad's mind. If Thad was feeling energetic, Tom would buck almost as hard as a raw bronc. If Thad didn't feel well, Tom would just give a few token crow-hops. Sometimes Tom wouldn't buck at all when Thad felt especially sickly. Man and horse had a rare bond.

So when Thad had looked the town over and surmised what he could, he decided to proceed down the main street. Almost as soon as he made the decision, almost before his boot heels gently touched Tom's side, the horse was moving forward. Something, probably, in the slight shifting of his master's weight, had telegraphed that information to the intelligent animal.

Thad dismounted and looped the reins around the hitch rail in front of the first saloon they came to. The sign over the door simply said, 'Saloon'. No name. Not that it mattered. The owner evidently had the same thought, so he just didn't bother tagging some pretentious name on to it.

Looking both ways again at the empty street, Thad shrugged through the front door. He paused briefly to let his eyes adjust to the dim interior. What he saw inside was a mirror of what he saw outside. Nothing. Conspicuous, inappropriate, incongruous nothing slapped against his senses.

The bartender looked up as he entered. His hand held a fairly clean towel with which he was polishing already clean glasses. Across the room a piano-player sat at a table with four women. All of the women were wearing too much rouge and lipstick. That was it. Not a customer in the place. None expected either, apparently.

Thad walked to the rough bar and planted a boot on the brass rail that ran along its base. 'What'll it be?' the bartender asked, his voice more cautious than courteous.

Something in the way he asked the routine question gave Thad the impression he was wary, as if expecting some sort of trouble. 'Whiskey,' he said, dropping a coin on the bar.

The bartender moved just a little too quickly to oblige. He poured a shot of whiskey, careful to fill the shot glass to within a whisker of the rim.

Thad lifted the over-filled glass carefully, and took a small sip. He waited for the glow to make its way to his stomach and begin to spread. He set the glass back down.

'That feels a whole lot better than trail dust,' he commented.

The bartender nodded, watching him carefully. 'Been a long ride?'

'Yup. It has.'

'Where'd you blow in from?'

'Started out in Lone Tree.'

The bartender's eyebrows rose. Thad had a sense that the man relaxed slightly. 'That's a good ways.'

When Thad didn't respond, he ventured, 'Headin' anywhere in particular?'

Thad shook his head. 'Lookin' for a fella.'

'You a lawman?'

'Not at the moment. I've been known to sport a badge a time or two. Could just as well be this trip, I s'pose.'

'Bounty huntin'?'

'Nope. Hired to find a woman-killer. I was hopin' maybe he'd holed up here. Or at least maybe somebody'd seen him.'

'What's he look like?'

'Young fella. 'Bout five-seven. Skinny. Ain't but about seventeen, eighteen years old. Sandy-haired. Blue-eyed. Quiet. Don't smile much.'

Thad didn't miss the quick glance the bartender shared with the group at the table. He knew with certainty he'd hit pay dirt. He waited for the bartender to acknowledge the fact.

The barkeep cleared his throat. 'That does sound like a guy that was here a while back. Maybe a week or so.'

'He stick around long?'

The bartender glanced at the table again, trying hard to not make it obvious. 'Nope. Don't guess so. Not here, anyway. Unless he hooked up with . . . uh . . . well, he might've drifted on down to Lefty's.'

'What's Lefty's?'

'That's the other saloon in town.'

'They busier than this one?'

The bartender shot a stronger glance toward the table. He glanced involuntarily at both the front and back doors. He lowered his voice a notch. 'Yeah, they got a lot more business. You might wanta be a bit circumspect about droppin' in there, though.'

'Does that have somethin' to do with why the town looks so dead?'

The bartender nodded, not bothering to look to the group at the table for support. 'There ain't too many folks 'round about comin' into Paradise for supplies these days.'

'Why not?'

'Most of 'em don't like the idea o' havin' to pay a toll on whatever they buy. Then the price of everything is higher than most places, 'cause the merchants have to pay a toll on it too.'

'Pay a toll to who?'

This time the bartender looked around again before he answered, as if to assure himself there were no extra ears listening. 'Paul Hogue and his boys.'

'Who's Paul Hogue? I've never heard of him.'

'Neither had we, till about a month ago. Him and his boys — eight of 'em — nine, countin' Hogue — rode in and kinda took over the town.'

'Really? I never heard of that happenin'. How'd they manage to take over a whole town?'

'They killed the town marshal and his deputy. When they announced they was takin' over the town, Dick and Henry came right after 'em. They didn't stand a chance. Hogue and his boys didn't even bother to talk. When Dick and Henry identified themselves, Hogue and a couple of his men just pulled leather and shot 'em all to pieces.'

'How to buffalo a whole town, right off the bat,' Thad muttered.

'They sure 'nuf got the job done. From then on everybody was afraid to stand up to 'em. They announced they were in charge of everything. From now on, there'll be a ten per cent toll on everything anyone bought in Paradise. That includes anything anyone sells someone else in town, or anything the blacksmith charges anyone, or the livery barn ... whatever it is, even the whiskey you just bought, has a ten per cent toll on it.'

'Paradise lost,' Thad muttered.

'Huh?'

'Never mind. Just thinkin'. Nobody's rode out to find a US marshal or anything?'

'Hank Redfern did. He didn't get far. He was shot in the back less than a mile outa town. Left to lay right there in the middle o' the road, after his pockets were emptied.'

'Any question about who killed him?'

The bartender looked around again before he answered. 'They made sure there wouldn't be no question about that. One of Hogue's men has been flashin' Hank's watch, ever since. Whenever anyone in town acts like they're gettin' tired o' the situation, one of 'em will ask Nevada, 'Hey, Nevada, what time is it?' Then Nevada'll make a big show o' pullin' out Hank's watch an' lookin' at it. Then he'll say, 'Why, I do believe it's time to make sure nobody in this town starts gettin' any crazy ideas.' That does the trick. Anyone knows if they resist, they'll get a bullet in the back just like Hank did.'

A slow anger began to stir in Thad. Even as it did, a competing voice within him scolded him. He wasn't here to help a townful of people too weak or timid to help themselves. He didn't need something slowing him down and making Long's trail even colder. It had already taken him far too long to even feel like he was on a warm enough trail to follow. Besides, this wasn't his fight.

At the same time his sense of fairness and decency boiled at the thought of fewer than a dozen men running roughshod over a whole town, brazenly cowing and fleecing it.

He sipped the whiskey slowly, thoughtfully. 'What are the townsfolk like?' he asked eventally.

The bartender shrugged. ' 'Bout the same as people everywhere, I guess. They're good folks, for the most part. Family folks.'

'How many of 'em have guns?'

'Oh, 'bout all of 'em, I'd guess. There ain't none of 'em what you'd call gun-handy, though. They hunt an' all such as that, but they ain't up to fightin' a war. Some of 'em was in the war, though.'

'How about the ranches around?

35

Surely they've got enough men to put a stop to this.'

'You'd think so. We keep waitin' for one or more of 'em to come ridin' in with a bunch of men and clean out that nest down at Lefty's. It ain't happened yet, though.'

Thad grunted in response. People who stood around waiting for someone else to solve their problems for them didn't earn a lot of respect in his mind. He mulled it over a while longer.

He addressed the bartender again. 'These townspeople. If they had someone leadin' 'em, tellin' and showin' 'em what to do, would they stand up to those guys?'

The bartender thought it over for quite a while. When he answered, his voice was firmer and more definite than Thad expected. 'Yeah. Yeah, they would. If it was somebody they trusted, at least. They're sick and tired of the situation as it is. They've either gotta get up the backbone to take care of it, or walk away from everything they've got here. Yeah, they'll fight, if they know how to go about it, and if they think they've got a chance to win. They wouldn't have, at first. They would now.'

'Then can you send someone around town to get the word out quietly? Have as many of 'em as will to come here? We'll see what we can do.'

A slow grin spread across the bartender's face. Before he could answer, one of the girls got up from the table. She was younger than the rest. Her dark hair looked natural. She wore much less powder and rouge than the rest. 'I'll do it,' she volunteered.

A mischievous glimmer sparkled in her eyes. One of those eyes showed the unmistakable colors of a several-day-old black eye. The deep purple of the bruise was turning green and yellow around the edges, as it healed. The size of the bruising indicated she had worn an exceptionally big shiner for a while. 'I've always wanted to knock on some of those doors anyway.'

Thad resisted the urge to smile. 'You might not wanta call any of the men by name,' he suggested.

She giggled as she turned to slip out the back door.

4

Thad chatted with the bartender as the sun lowered and shadows lengthened. When it grew too dim to see easily in the room, the bartender went about the place, lighting the lamps. The smell of burnt matches and coal oil competed with stale beer and whiskey for dominance.

Millie, as Thad learned the young 'working girl's' name was, returned within an hour of when she had gone. She slipped back in the back door as quietly as she had left. She said nothing. She just rejoined the others at the table.

Just after dark, the first people began to arrive. They slid furtively in the back door, looking around nervously. As others arrived, they grouped at the end of the bar, eyeing Thad nervously, talking amongst themselves in muted tones.

When more than a dozen were assembled, Thad stepped away from the bar. He spoke to the table of the saloon's permanent denizens. 'One of you might want a keep a lookout at the front door. Another one at the rear. Just in case some of Hogue's men notice folks slippin' in here.'

Millie and another woman rose immediately. Millie posted herself at the back door. The older, harder-looking one, took the front door. She opened it just enough to peer carefully up and down the street. Then, seeming to think better of the idea, she opened the door wide and positioned herself in it, as if making herself conspicuous. She leaned backward against the side of the door-frame. She carefully arranged her skirt to expose an ankle, advertising for business.

A slight smile played at the corners of Thad's mouth as he silently approved the tactic. She was now in a position to see anything that moved on the street, without appearing in any way furtive or suspicious.

Thad turned to face the group of men who eyed him expectantly. 'My name's Thad Palmer,' he said.

Before he could continue, a voice from the group said, 'From Kansas?'

Thad's eyebrows rose. His reply was cautious. 'I've been in Kansas.'

'I've heard of you,' the other said. He stepped to the front of the group. 'My brother's got a place in Kansas. He's told me about you bein' brung in by some small ranchers there when a range war was brewin'. A couple big ranches was tryin' to steal everything the little guys had worked for years to build. He's told me stories about you that don't seem rightly possible.'

'They probably aren't,' Thad disclaimed at once. 'Folks like to make a story a little better each time they tell it.'

'He says you're hell on high red wheels in a fight.'

Normally it irritated Thad that his reputation followed, and sometimes preceded him, wherever he went. It made it virtually impossible to get any kind of job except as a gunman or a lawman.

At the present, however, he decided it might be a definite advantage. His reputation might serve to infuse the town's populace with at least some of the courage they would surely need. 'I haven't met a man yet who could stand against me,' he said quietly.

He gave his words time to soak in, then continued. 'How many of you boys own a shotgun?' he asked the group.

As if they were schoolboys responding to a teacher's question, half a dozen hands went up.

'Do you have ammunition for 'em?'

All nodded. 'One thing a lot of people don't understand. Especially in close quarters, like inside a saloon, a shotgun's worth any three gunmen with pistols. You don't have to aim well. You don't have to draw quick. You just have to point and shoot, and a shotgun makes an awful hole in a man at close range.'

Again he gave his words time to soak in. 'How many of you are halfway decent with a pistol?'

This time every hand in the group went up.

A stir from the back door caught everybody's instant attention. A grubby old man shambled in, his bleary eyes casting about the room. 'Looks like some sorta meetin' goin' on,' he observed.

'C'mon in, Weepy,' the bartender invited. 'Have a drink. On the house.'

The old drunk licked his lips. He cast another glance around the room. He was not capable of concealing the fact that he was counting heads, memorizing names. He looked back at the bartender. 'Well, maybe just one, Bub,' he said. 'Then I gotta go.'

'Where is it that you've gotta go to, Weepy?' one of the men asked immediately.

Weepy looked around as if wishing for a rabbit warren to duck into. Instead of responding, he grabbed the shot of whiskey the bartender had placed on the bar. He downed it in a quick gulp, set the shot glass on the bar, and headed for the back door.

One of the men grabbed him by the arm. 'Hold it, Weepy! Where you goin' in such a hurry?'

'We all know exactly where he's goin'. I'll betcha ten to one he's headin' for Lefty's to tell Hogue we're up to somethin',' another spoke up.

Weepy looked around like a cornered rat, seeking an avenue of escape.

Thad took a deep breath. 'Weepy, do you see that table over there?'

The increasingly frantic man looked over at the piano-player and the women at the table with him. He nodded his head silently.

Thad said, 'You go over there and sit down. About every half hour or so, Bub'll send you a shot of whiskey. If you get off that chair, Bub will use the shotgun he keeps under the bar to blow your guts all over the room. Do you understand that?'

In response to Thad's words, the bartender reached under the bar. He pulled out a sawed-off double-barreled shotgun and laid it on top of the bar in front of him.

Weepy's face turned a pasty white. He cast desperately around the room for support, but saw none in the faces staring him down. 'But, but what if I gotta go take a leak?'

'Well, you'll have your choice, Weepy. You can hold it, you can sit there and wet your pants, or you can try to get out the door and see if you can move fast enough to outrun a load of buckshot.'

One of the men reached out and took hold of the now trembling barfly. He propelled him toward the designated table with a shove. Weepy staggered, fighting to keep his balance. One of the women stood up and grabbed him, slamming him down onto a chair so hard it rattled his teeth.

Thad turned back to the men. 'OK, men. Here's the plan. It's simple. It'll work, if every man does his part. If you don't, I'll be dead and Hogue will kill at least half of you as an example to the rest of the town.'

He briefly sketched out a plan. As it unfolded, men began to look at one another and nod. It was so straightforward and simple, at least half of them wondered why nobody had thought of it sooner.

When everyone had his questions answered, they all slipped out the back door as silently as they had come.

Thad waited fully half an hour. Then he walked out the front door, mounted his horse, and rode the short block to Lefty's. He dismounted there, again looping the reins of his horse over the hitchrail. He noted that in spite of the sounds of activity inside, there were no other horses at the rail. That meant everyone inside was already living in town, or planning to stay awhile.

He stepped through the front door and paused while his eyes adjusted. Every eye in the place darted to him.

A couple of the occupants casually dropped their hands to the immediate vicinity of their gun butts.

Thad looked around, then strode to the bar. He tossed a coin on the bar. 'Whiskey,' he said.

The bartender obliged, watching him closely. Thad noticed he wasn't nearly as careful to give full measure for the money as the bartender at the other saloon. The shot glass was scarcely more than half full.

He took a small sip, then turned and hooked an elbow on the bar. 'This looks more like it,' he said, his voice casually friendly as he looked sidelong at the bartender. 'I stopped at the other saloon on the way into town. It seemed more like a morgue than a saloon.'

The bartender laughed just a trifle too heartily. 'They don't do much business these days,' he agreed.

'At least there's music and some women who look like they'd at least like to take a couple dollars from a lonesome cowboy here.'

'Just hit town, huh?'

Fully aware someone would have noticed his horse at the other saloon, he said, 'Just a little bit ago. Bought a drink at the other place, but it was just way too quiet in there for me. Not very friendly, either. They acted like they were even afraid to talk to me.'

'Plan on stayin' long?'

'Nope. Plan on gettin' me a room. I wanta sleep in a decent bed one night at least, before I go back to sleepin' on the ground.'

'The ground can get a little hard all right.'

'Gets right lonesome, too.'

'It does that.'

'You got rooms upstairs?'

'For all night?'

'Yup.'

'Sure. Fifty cents. Unless you want company.'

'I sure don't wanta sleep alone. I can do that in the bunkhouse. What's that gal's name that's sittin' by herself over there?'

He jutted his chin toward one of the saloon girls, sitting alone at a table near the piano. 'That's Sally.'

'She do all-nighters?'

'Sure. For the right price.'

'What's the right price?'

'Depends. She'll let you know.'

Thad nodded, tossing another coin onto the bar. 'How about a glass of whatever Sally likes.'

He was smart enough to know that the bottle the bartender filled another glass with was tea. That was fine. He really didn't care. He picked it up and carried it, along with his own drink, to the table where Sally sat alone.

'Pardon me, ma'am,' he said as he stopped across the table from her. 'Would a lonesome gentleman be able to buy you a drink? You look about as lonesome as I feel, sittin' here by yourself.'

She looked him up and down appraisingly. His appearance obviously appealed to her. 'Sure. I could use a drink,' she acknowledged. 'Sit down.'

'Thank you,' he offered as he sat down. He sat the drink the bartender had poured for her on the table in front of her. He took off his hat and turned it bottom side up on the table.

'You look like you've ridden a ways.'

'I have for a fact,' he agreed. 'Too far, and too lonesome.'

'Some men like being alone.'

'Not all the time. Not me, anyway. Especially at night. I don't mind sleepin' on the ground that much. I just hate doin' it alone.'

'Not many women want to sleep on the ground.'

'That's why I try to find a nice friendly town to stay overnight in once in a while.'

She smiled at him and took a sip of her drink. Her eyes locked on his over the rim of the glass. Without lowering it, she said, 'If I didn't know better, I might think this was leading up to a proposition.'

'Would it interest you if it were?'

Her eyes danced briefly. 'Well now, it

just might. Depends on just how lonesome you are, and whether you want company for a little while or the whole night.'

He smiled back at her. 'Well, what might be a reasonable exchange for the whole night?'

'You need a bath and a shave,' she announced abruptly.

He grinned openly. 'I sure do, on both counts. Is that included?'

'You'd trust me to shave you?'

'Are you handy with a razor?'

'Honey, I'm handy with everything you're apt to care about.'

'Well then, let's go for the whole shebang.'

He noticed, without appearing to pay attention, that all of the saloon's patrons had returned to what they were doing when he entered. In their minds, his presence was explained, his actions were routine, and he merited no further concern.

'Ten dollars,' Sally responded.

His eyebrows rose. 'Are you really worth all that?'

Her eyes genuinely sparkled for the first sign of any real emotion since he had sat down. 'I'll tell you what, honey. If you don't think so in the morning, I'll give you half of it back.'

'Well now, a money-back guarantee is something I've never heard of before.'

'Honey, you ain't been with Sally before, either.'

He nodded his agreement. He hauled a ten-dollar gold piece out of his pocket and slid it across the table. 'You get that bath water ready. I need to go take care of my horse. I'll be back in fifteen minutes. What room will I find you in?'

'Number seven. Your lucky number. Top of the stairs, third door on the right.'

'Number seven it is,' he replied. He hoped she'd interpret the almost untouched glass of whiskey he left on the table as a sign of his eagerness to get to the room.

5

Thad handed Tom's reins to the hostler at the livery barn. 'He could use a bait o' grain, along with some hay and water,' he said.

'He need the water slow?'

'Naw, he should be fine.'

'How long you leavin' 'im?'

'Just overnight, most likely.'

'That'll be sixty cents.'

Thad's eyebrows rose in feigned surprise. 'That's a bit more than most places.'

The hostler shrugged his unwillingness to discuss it. 'Our costs went up some,' he mumbled.

Thad looked at him a brief moment, then untied his bedroll. He lifted it and his saddle-bags from the saddle. 'He oughta get a good rubdown too, for that price.'

The hostler muttered something

incoherent as he led Tom toward a stall.

Thad slung the saddle-bags over his left shoulder, then threw his bedroll over the same shoulder. That left his right hand free to hover above his gun butt. At the corner of the livery barn he paused as if looking up and down the street. Without moving his head, he asked softly, 'Everybody set?'

He was relieved to hear an instant answer, just as soft, from the shadows. 'All set. Several more fellas than what you met. Half of 'em are hid out behind Lefty's. The other half are between buildings on both sides, ready to head in the front door when you give the signal.'

'You're gonna be where you can hear me?'

'How much time you need, once you go back in?'

Thad did some quick mental calculations. 'Give me fifteen minutes from right now.'

'We'll be right close to both doors, listenin'.'

With no further exchange, Thad crossed the street and walked toward Lefty's. At the empty space between Lefty's and the store next to it, he detected the presence of several people. He hoped they did a better job once they were inside than they did keeping quiet enough to not be noticed by anyone walking by.

He stopped just outside the door, where lamplight made a yellow almost-rectangle on the board sidewalk. In its glow, he consulted his pocket watch. He allowed just about a minute for his walk from the livery barn.

He re-entered the front door of the saloon. Once again, all eyes turned to him immediately. They just as quickly recognized him, and dismissed him from their concern. Mentally he sized up those he guessed were Paul Hogue's men. From among those, he had already singled out one in particular as he had gone through the necessary flirtation with Sally.

He had a pinched face and a

hawklike nose. His mouth had a particularly callous twist as he talked to the man standing next to him at the bar. He wore a well-worn Colt low on his left hip, and his left hand never strayed very far from it. He stood so that side was always clear of the bar. He wore a low-crowned hat, typical of cowboys from a long way south and west of Wyoming. He was still standing that way as Thad returned. He was willing to bet that would be the one called 'Nevada'.

He walked up the stairs, taking pains to look and act eager for what waited there. He walked down the hall and stopped in front of the door with a brass '7' nailed to the casing. He started to knock, when Sally's voice called, 'C'mon on in, honey. You took seventeen minutes. I was beginning to wonder if I'd been stood up.'

Thad swung the door inward and stepped in. Wearing only bloomers and a bodice, Sally stood behind a bathtub of steaming water. 'Peel them clothes off and climb in, cowboy,' she invited. 'Sally'll have you feeling like a new man in no time.'

Thad studied her face a long moment, hoping he had sized her up right. 'That'll have to wait,' he announced.

Her eyes grew suddenly cautious, fearful. 'What're you talking about?'

'How much would you like to get rid of Hogue and his boys?'

Her eyes reflected stark terror for one brief moment. It was replaced almost at once with what he thought was a glimmer of hopefulness. 'What are you talking about?'

'Can I trust you?'

Her eyes grew cautious again. 'That depends.'

'OK. I'll take a chance and level with you. In almost exactly ten minutes, all hell's gonna bust loose downstairs. Can you get the word to the other girls to hit the floor as soon as it does? I don't want anyone but Hogue's men gettin' shot up.'

'Who are you? Why are you doing this?'

'There ain't no part o' time to explain all that. Are you gonna side with us, or do I have to hogtie you and gag you to keep you outa trouble?'

She studied him for a long minute, her eyes hard. Then she said, 'I'd give up my left one to get rid of that bunch.'

'Then you got four minutes to figure out how to get word to the other girls without tippin' off Hogue or any of his boys.'

She gave him one more searching look, then hurried out the door. He heard her softly rap on the door of the next room. A brief exchange of softly spoken words were followed by somebody's footsteps heading swiftly toward the steps. Sally came right back into the room. 'I sent Lily down to do it. If I showed up, they'd all wonder how you got done with me so quick.'

He nodded and consulted his watch. He walked out into the hallway and walked softly to near the head of the stairs. Staying where he was unlikely to be seen, he watched as Lily, seemingly with bored detachment, stopped and whispered something into the ear of one of the girls. The girl's eyes widened. She glanced briefly toward the steps, then returned her attention to the man across the table from her.

Thad consulted his watch again. Two more minutes.

He moved to where he could see Nevada. Mentally, he placed the one he was certain would be Hogue, planning exactly how to target the ringleader of the bunch with what he hoped would be his second shot. After his challenge of Nevada, Hogue would almost certainly be standing.

One more minute.

He listened closely to the low murmur of conversation. It seemed to him as if there was more chatter from the girls, just a little too loud. To him, it sounded as if they were deliberately trying to distract as many as possible from his expected presence.

Maybe they were all as eager as Sally to be rid of what was almost certainly the brutality of Hogue's men, and their destruction of the normal business traffic in Paradise Corner. He certainly hoped that was the case.

Of course, it could just as easily be an elevated level of noise to disguise a message being sent to Hogue to alert him. He would know within thirty seconds.

He waited what he was almost certain was long enough. As he stepped to the top of the stairs and started down, he caught just a brief hint of movement beyond the front door. 'A little eager, but they're there,' he silently assured himself.

He was on the bottom step, when he stopped. He called out, in a louder voice than was necessary, 'Hey Nevada! You wanta tell me what time it is?'

The working girls all began making their way as swiftly as possible to a wall, out of the line of expected fire. All other eyes in the place swiveled to him and locked there. As a result, nobody but the working girls saw the line of men walk swiftly in the front door and range along the front wall.

Out of the range of his vision, Thad was hopefully optimistic that the same thing was occurring along the rear wall.

Nevada stepped away from the bar, his left hand touching the well-worn handle of his Colt. He had guessed the identity of Nevada right. 'Who are you?' he demanded.

'Just a real man that can't stand yellow-bellied back-shooters.'

Nevada was quite possibly the fastest man with a gun Thad had ever seen. He gambled that the man would draw just as he finished the last word of his challenge, and he was already drawing his own gun, with speed that easily matched the outlaw's. The gamble just barely gave him the edge he needed.

His own forty-five roared a split second before Nevada's. The leaden projectile slammed into the outlaw's chest, driving him backward enough to send his own shot just wide of Thad.

Wood slivers flew from the stair banister just beside him.

With no hesitation, Thad took a swift, long step down onto the saloon's floor and whirled. His second shot caught Hogue squarely in the chest just as he was drawing his own gun.

Instantly the roar of a dozen shotguns thundered from both the front and rear of the saloon. All but two of Hogue's men either crumpled forward or were propelled backward by loads of buckshot. Several of them had taken multiple wads of the hot lead.

In the unearthly silence that followed the deafening roar, the surviving two threw up their hands. Almost as if it came from one voice, they yelled, 'Don't shoot!'

Even the bartender backed against the rows of bottles on the back-bar, his hands flung high in the air, his face pasty white.

It was over just that quickly. Thad surveyed the room quickly, looking for holdouts. He spotted Sally at the top of the stairs. 'Any of 'em upstairs?' he demanded.

'There's only two men up here,' she announced. 'Both cowboys gettin' rid of their wages. None of Hogue's men.'

Thad turned to the row of men, nervously but triumphantly holding shotguns, still leveled at the room. 'You boys might oughta lower them barrels a ways,' he suggested.

As if suddenly wakened from some impossible dream, they all hastened to do so.

'Which one of you'd make the best actin' town marshal?' he inquired.

The townsmen looked at one another. Then several of them fixed their gaze on one man. He acknowledged their silent nomination. 'I guess I could do that, for the time bein',' he said.

Thad nodded. 'Then it looks like you're it. Some of you fellas can take the two still standin' and lock 'em up. You got your town back.'

Without waiting for a response, he walked back up the stairs. Sally followed him to room number seven. When he walked in and picked up his bedroll and saddle-bags, she looked surprised, then confused. 'You ain't leavin', are you?'

He looked at her, fighting the feelings that surged within him. 'Yeah, I guess so. Sorry to take advantage of you that way. I had to have a way to get things set up without tippin' my hand too quick.'

She nodded her understanding of that. 'I understand that. But you already got the night paid for,' she reminded him. 'You oughta at least stick around for the bath and the shave.'

He decided that wouldn't be all that bad an idea. Then he thought about whether there might be some who were loyal to Hogue still out there somewhere. He also knew if he stayed here, it wouldn't stop with a bath and a shave. It wouldn't be a very good idea to be that totally distracted in the heart of what had been, until moments ago, the outlaws' headquarters.

'I 'spect that'll have to wait till another time,' he said.

She stepped up in front of him. She slid his ten-dollar gold piece into his pants pocket. 'Then here's your money back. And you got a freebie comin' any time you wanta come back.'

He didn't want to admit how inviting that sounded, or how difficult it was to shoulder his things and walk out.

6

He was suddenly tired. Very, very tired. He only wanted to get to Paradise Corner's only real hotel, get a room, prop a chair under the doorknob, and get some sleep.

His bedroll and saddle-bags seemed heavier than he remembered. He knew the threat he'd sensed waiting for him here was all over. Even so, he kept the bedroll and saddle-bags on his left shoulder, his right hand always free to reach his gun. It was a long walk, that half a block to the hotel.

He was almost there, directly across the street from the saloon he had first entered. Lamplight spilled into the street briefly as the door opened and closed. His hand instinctively grabbed his gun, drawing it halfway out of the holster.

'Hey, don't shoot me! I'm on your

side, remember?' A lilting feminine voice managed to sound light and almost teasing, in spite of the fear that tinged the edges of her words.

Thad recognized Millie, the gutsy little working girl who had summoned the townsmen to the meeting that set his impromptu plan in motion.

He stopped, facing the young woman. 'It's all over, Millie. I owe you a big thanks. So does the town. You sure enough knew what men to get to that meetin'.'

She nodded, her expression indecipherable in the wash of the full moon. 'I do know men,' she said. 'Where are you headin' now?'

'Over to the hotel. I gotta get some sleep.'

'Sleep all you're needin'?'

'At the moment, yeah, I guess it is.'

'I have a room at the back of the saloon. It ain't fancy, but it's clean. It comes with benefits the room at the hotel doesn't. Besides, it won't cost you nothin'. I owe you, for cleanin' out that nest of maggots.'

Thad fought to think of a response. Twice inside the space of an hour he had been offered free 'services' by an unusually attractive saloon girl. He felt the weight of fatigue lift from his shoulders, as the appeal of her offer stirred in him.

He mentally shook his head. 'Now that's an offer that's awful hard to turn down,' he said. 'You are one fine looking woman. You got a lot of grit. I'm just as indebted to you. But I guess I'll be goin' on to the hotel.'

He could feel, as much as see, the instant umbrage in her posture. 'What? You don't take up with whores?'

He hesitated, struggling to frame the words of an answer that wouldn't further offend her.

'Never mind,' she said. The bitterness in her voice was not in the least disguised. 'You answered well enough by not answering.'

'I got nothin' against you,' he stumbled, his response sounding lame, even to himself.

'Yeah, I know. You just don't do whores. Even though every other woman is just as much a whore as I am. I'm just honest about it.'

He knew he was tired, but her words weren't making sense. 'What do you mean?'

The flow of her words clearly indicated how often she had thought through the conviction — or the rationalization — that she put into words. 'Think about it. Every woman that gets married makes the same deal I make with any man I take money from. She agrees to spread her legs for him, in exchange for what's in it for her. She wants a place to live. She wants some nice stuff. She wants security. Whatever it is she wants, she agrees to satisfy him as long as he gives her what she wants. She's giving herself to him in exchange for what she wants, just the same as I do. If she don't get what she wants from him, he don't get what he wants from her. So I'm really no different from every married woman in the world.'

Thad thought of several responses. He could just turn and walk away. He could at least appear to agree. Somehow he couldn't make himself do either one. He struggled for the words to respond. 'There is a difference,' he replied finally. 'Yeah, that's part of marriage, I agree. But it's only part. Part of it is also the agreement that they keep that between just the two of them. Neither of them looks for that in someone else.'

'Yeah, right,' she retorted. 'That's why I make such good money. Half my customers are married men.'

'I'm sure that's true,' he conceded. 'But that don't make it right. That don't make it part of what's supposed to be. That's a violation of that marriage agreement, and it's wrong. And there's more to that agreement than sleepin' together. When folks get married, they promise to take care of each other, whether they're sick or hurt or just feelin' frisky. They agree to share the work and the heartaches and the risks and the pain. They agree to win the battles they win together, and lose the ones they lose together. They agree to face whatever else comes along as a team, doin' it together. Maybe the most important, they agree to raise their kids together, givin' them the kind of home that'll make 'em turn out to be good folks when they grow up. It's all a package deal, and I 'spect that's the way things is supposed to be. Takin' care of what each other needs in the bedroom's just part of it.'

She opened her mouth twice, then a third time, to reply, and closed it again. Finally, in a voice much smaller than he had heard from her before, she said, 'Some woman down the road's gonna be awful lucky to hook up with you. Where I live, I don't find many like that.'

'I guess that's what most guys hope for,' was all he could think of to respond.

She started to turn away, then turned back. 'Oh, that guy you're hunting?'

'Yeah?'

'He's the one that gave me this shiner.'

'He hit you?'

She nodded. 'Nailed me a good one. I went to my room with him, and things was goin' along like normal. Only then, he couldn't do nothin'. It wouldn't work.'

He didn't know how to respond, so he didn't. She continued. 'Then he got real mad. Started cussin' a blue streak. Called me some things even I hadn't heard before. Then he up and slugged me. Hard. Knocked me back on the bed. Almost knocked me out, but not quite. Then he worked just fine.'

The import of what she was telling him slowly sunk in. 'But he had to hurt you first.'

She nodded. 'He had to hurt me first. He didn't feel like enough of a man until he hurt me. You said he's already killed one woman. I guess I was lucky. I just got a black eye. But he's gonna kill a lot more women if you don't find him.'

She turned and walked across the street. He stood and watched her until she disappeared through the door of the saloon. A deep sadness he couldn't explain settled like a heavy blanket over him.

He shrugged his shoulders. He took a deep breath. He slouched the rest of the way to the hotel. He got a room, propped the chair under the doorknob, fell onto the bed and dropped almost immediately into a deep, exhausted sleep.

He was up with the sun the next morning. He washed, shaved, and ate breakfast in the hotel's dining room. He retrieved Tom from the livery barn and rode out of town.

He pulled the reins, stopping Tom dead in his tracks. At the edge of town, right beside the road, a massive cottonwood spread its branches. Moving ever so slightly in the breeze, two men hung from the branches of the great tree.

'Don't look like the two that survived the saloon even made it to the lockup,' Thad muttered.

He nudged Tom forward, past the macabre symbol of swift justice. 'Probably just as well,' he informed his horse. 'I 'spect they needed hangin' as much as the fella we're huntin'.'

7

Dust hung in the still air. Its acrid taste filled every cowhand's mouth. It formed tiny balls of mud at the corners of the eyes, next to the nose. It coated everything.

Twenty mustangs, ears laid back, eyes wide, nostrils flaring, trotted in circles around the large corral, seeking an avenue of escape.

Four cowboys sat their horses outside the just-closed gate, inside the wings of fence that angled outward from it. Those fences had the effect of funneling the wild horses into the gate, before they were able to see that it had already cut off their escape in both directions.

The fifth cowboy stood at the gate, where he had just secured it.

'Them's some fine animals.' One of them put the thoughts of all into words.

The other four nodded their agreement.

'I wanta put my brand on that young stud,' the newest member of the crew announced.

The others eyed him appraisingly.

He had only been part of the crew a couple weeks. He'd ridden into the ranch just as they were getting ready for a wild-horse drive. They had spent a month building a sturdy corral, and the wing fences that stretched in a broadening V for a good quarter mile. Those wing fences were carefully built into, through, and behind every clump of sage brush, chokecherry bush, and tree that was close enough to utilize. They used whatever would mask the fence until the horses were well within jaws that would squeeze them inexorably to and through the corral's gate. Even that was disguised with brush, so they wouldn't realize the nature of the trap until they were beyond it. From their view, as they surged through that gate, the opening would appear as an escape route from the narrowing confines of the wing fences.

One of the greatest problems with capturing wild horses was how to get them to water while they were still too wild to control. They had solved that problem by building the corral across a small stream, so that fresh water would be available to the horses at all times. The spot also had abundant grass, which would suffice for a time. By the time they had eaten or trampled it beyond use, they would either be capable of being picketed on grass or they could be fed hay thrown over the fence.

They all knew where this particular herd of wild horses they wanted to capture was currently grazing. They had been watching their movements all spring. When calving was over, they had turned to building the corral where it would be feasible to drive the herd into its trap.

There was some immediate resentment when the young man had ridden in and hired on. Calving was a hard, sleep-depriving, demanding time on a ranch. Special vigilance was necessary around the clock during calving. It was a perilous time for cows with breached calves. Predators always targeted new-born calves for the tasty meal too young to flee. Those and a dozen other things could erase a ranch's profits for the year in a matter of days.

Now that was behind them. The wild-horse drive would be a lark, a reward, a celebration. The ranch needed the horses to augment their remuda. Every cowboy would have a chance to break horses for his own string. If he found one he especially liked, the rancher might well sell it to him for his private horse. Plus they had the recreation of watching everyone else try to 'top off' a wild horse for the first time.

That this newcomer should arrive right after all the hard work, and share in the time they all regarded as a reward, seemed patently unfair. He proved himself a hard worker though. He was agreeable to work with. He pulled his weight and more in the finishing touches on the corral. They had begun to accept him as part of the crew.

He proved especially adept on the drive itself. As luck would have it, a couple young studs, bent on challenging the established stud of the herd, were close to the rest when the drive began. They were crowded into the herd. It was a rarity to ever capture more than one stud, other than young colts, with a herd. This time they had three.

'Which one?' the straw boss asked.

'The black.'

The ranch foreman studied the horse in question. 'He's a good four or five years old. He'll be a handful to ride.'

The young cowboy grinned. 'Yeah, I figured that. He'll make a fine horse, though.'

The foreman nodded. 'If he ain't too studdy.'

The youngster's grin just broadened. 'I'm bettin' I can handle 'im.'

The straw boss studied him for a long moment, then nodded his head. 'I 'spect it's as good a time as any to find out. They're wore down some from drivin' 'em in. You'n Shakey can drop a couple ropes on 'im, and drag 'im out.'

The cowboy manning the gate immediately lifted the wire loop holding it and opened it enough to allow the two mounted men to enter. The youngster shook out a loop in his lariat, then started easing along the corralled horses. They began to run in a circle around him. He stayed close, but not close enough to interrupt the flow of their movements, watching for his chance.

The black stud veered away from the outside of the corral, moving to get around a mare in front of him that was moving too slowly. As he did, he was isolated for a brief moment on the side of the bunch next to the two cowboys. The youngster's rope shot forward from his hand instantly, its loop settling over the stud's neck before the horse knew it was even close. Just as the loop passed over the stud's head, the youngster jerked hard on the rope, closing the loop. At the same instant his own horse set his feet. The rope hummed taut with a jerk.

As the rope touched the stud, he reacted instantly. Nearly jerked off his feet, he spun around, facing the source of the strange thing that had grasped his neck. As it jerked tight again, he emitted a squeal of fear and anger. He reared against it, as the second loop, from the other cowboy settled over his head as well.

With both ropes straining against him, he reared, lunged, and fought.

Both cowboys began to back their straining horses toward the gate. The stud fought against their movement, but the two horses were too strong a force for him to resist. He was pulled away from the other horses.

The stricture of the ropes deprived him of air as well. As he pulled back against their force, he became more and more desperate to breathe. The cowboys watched him closely. His eyes began to bulge. His tongue came out. As it became apparent that he was losing strength, they both nudged their horses forward.

The ropes both went slightly slack. The stud stood glaring at them, spraddle-legged, sucking in great gulps of air.

As soon as his breathing approached normal, he lunged back against the ropes again. The two captors began backing their horses again, drawing ever closer to the gate.

Once more they had to stop and let the stud catch his breath. Then they were through the gate and it was secured behind them.

The two riders spread their horses further apart, making a two-way pull on the lariats. That restricted the stud from lunging to either side. Another cowboy shook out a small loop in his own lariat. Riding close, he whirled the loop around his head once and let it fly, twisting his wrist as he released it. The loop sailed toward the ground just in front of the stud's prancing hindlegs.

Just as it arrived, it turned over as if it had a mind of its own. The prancing hindleg of the horse was snared in the loop as cleverly as if he had stepped in a loop snare laid out on the ground. The cowboy jerked the loop tight.

Riding close to the stud, he flipped the rope so it flopped up over the stud's back. He rode forward until he was even with the stud's head, and dismounted. Hauling on his rope, he lifted the stud's hind leg forward and up, bringing it up almost against his stomach.

Now the stud could neither kick him, nor turn his head around to bite him. He flipped the rope around the base of the horse's neck and tied it with a loop that could be released with a pull on the end of the rope.

As soon as he had the hindleg tied up, he reached behind his saddle. He pulled a length of old blanket free. He folded it into a long strip, then reached out and flipped it over the stud's head. He pulled it over his eyes and tied the ends together beneath his jaw. The blindfolded stud stood on three legs, unable to move, trembling with fright and anger.

The other two released the tension on their lariats immediately. They removed their loops, coiled the ropes, and fastened them back onto the pommels of their saddles, buckling the leather straps that held them in readiness there.

The foreman addressed the young cowboy who had asked for the chance to ride the stud. 'Here.'

He tossed a hackamore toward him. The youngster snagged it out of the air and swiftly buckled it on the stud. He stripped the saddle from his own horse, and threw it onto the wild one. The wild horse shuddered under the foreign feel of its weight, but blindfolded and with one foot tied up, he could do nothing else.

The youngster removed the saddle-bags, his bedroll, his lariat, and his rifle from his saddle, piling them carefully on the ground. He removed the tools peculiar to a cowboy's needs from the container — made from the top of a worn-out boot — that was fastened to the side of the saddle. Then he stepped into the saddle. He settled into the saddle, savoring the stud's trembling beneath him. He measured just the right amount of rein and got a firm grip. He pulled his hat down clear onto his ears. 'Let 'im go, boys,' he said.

The blindfold was jerked off and the hindleg released in almost the same instant. The stud's nostrils flared. His eyes rolled. He exploded with a squeal of rage and fear, soaring several feet straight up.

He landed with a bone-jarring jolt. With no hesitation, he began to buck violently, squealing out his rage. He twisted and turned. He sunfished, side-jumped, reared and whirled. He bucked until the rider's head and neck had snapped back and forth so much that the cowboy couldn't see anything but a haze of red.

The youngster kept his toes turned

outward, his spurs hung in the cinch. He held on to the reins with a death grip. He kept his knees tightly clenched under the swells of the pommel. He tried to anticipate the direction of each twist and turn of the horse, to maintain his balance.

'Now there is a horseman,' one of the other cowboys commented as he watched.

'Rides that cayuse like he's glued to it,' a second affirmed.

'Looks like you hired yourself a horse wrangler,' the third said to the foreman.

'He can sure ride,' the foreman agreed.

The stud began to tire. His jumps began to be shorter and not as high. He began to telegraph more clearly the direction of his next lunge.

The rider began to relax perceptibly as well. He reached up with his free hand and pulled his hat loose from around his ears. He lifted it high over his head and yelled, 'Eeeee-haaa.'

He slapped the horse on the rump

with it. At the unexpected sound and slap, the stud renewed the frenzy of his bucking, but he was clearly out of hope of unseating the creature that sat astride him. He stopped abruptly, once again standing spraddle-legged. His rider would have none of it.

He spurred the tired horse abruptly, startling him into a run. As he ran, he felt himself being pulled by the reins, against his will, into a circle. He fought in vain against the pull of the rein, then yielded to it, turning that direction as he ran.

As soon as he yielded to it, the reins jerked the other way, forcing him to reverse the direction of his flight.

Back and forth, back and forth, around and around, then around and around the other way, the insistent, unshakable dictates of the accursed leather straps began more and more readily to control his movements.

When his tormentor decided it was time, he was forced back to the vicinity of the other men, then hauled to a stop by the strong pull on those reins. He stood once again, sides heaving, head down, spraddle-legged against his utter fatigue.

The cowboy leaped from his back. He came around in front of the stud. He talked in soothing tones. He rubbed beneath the straps of the hackamore, up the sides of his face, around his ears, under his chin.

At first the stud shied away, eyes rolling, ears back, snorting fearfully through flared nostrils. At the soothing sounds of the man's voice and the soft touch, he slowly began to relax. He found himself actually enjoying the scratching around the base of his ears.

'Here,' one of the cowboys said.

He handed the rider his hat, filled half full with water from his canteen.

The rider took the hat and held it where the horse could smell the water. He shied from the smell of the hat, but smelled the water as well. As it stayed there, just beneath his nose, his thirst finally got the better of his fear. He nuzzled the water carefully, and tossed his head. Then he reached his nose back into the hat and drank it dry.

'You are gonna make me one fine horse,' Vince Long exulted. 'Ain't you, Midnight?'

Midnight was far too spent to respond, as his new master began to unsaddle him and walk him around to cool him off before he rubbed him down.

8

A week of topping-off raw broncs left the small crew exhausted and irritable. At the same time, it was exhilarating. The horses were already beginning to respond well. Two of the mares were obviously horses that had been ridden at one time, prior to escaping to join a wild herd. They gentled quickly. One of the hands was already using one mare as part of his regular string.

Vince spent part of every day working with the black stud. He was a magnificent animal. He gentled far more quickly than anyone would have expected, under the skilled handling of the young Vince Long.

At the end of the week they took a break. They spent a couple days checking on cows and calves. Then they spent another day doing little but resting.

The following day, Vince and Shaky rode out together to check a bunch of cows they hadn't accounted for the previous couple days.

That was the day Thad Palmer rode into the ranch yard. The westering sun was snuggling down behind the distant mountains for a night's rest. Frogs in a beaver dam a quarter mile below the ranch yard filled the still air with their lullaby to the bedding sun. A sandpiper vied with a meadowlark for song dominance, the shrill tones of the sandpiper seeming incongruent with the melodious 'Oh gee Whilikers' sound of the meadowlark.

In spite of the serenity of the setting, Thad's nerves were as taut as fiddle strings. He had been following leads, trying to track Vince Long's movements after he had left Paradise Corner. The information that sent him to the Flying V L seemed pretty solid. A hand on a neighboring ranch told him about meeting a young cowboy who had hired on with the Flying V L. He had shown up at just about the right time. He exactly fit Thad's description. Thad had smiled drily several times as he thought of the irony of his quarry's hiring on with a ranch whose brand mimicked his initials.

As he rode cautiously into the yard, Vic Larsen stepped out onto the veranda of the house. He yelled at the barking dogs to silence them. 'Howdy,' he called as Thad approached. 'Git down and come in. I'm Vic Larsen.'

Thad dismounted, dropping Tom's reins onto the ground. He knew the horse would stay there as if tied until he was told to move. He strode to the rancher and gripped the extended hand. 'Evenin'. Fine day. I'm Thad Palmer.'

'You a lawman?'

Thad looked closely at him. 'Nope. Why do you ask?'

'You carry yourself like one. Either that or a gun-fighter.'

Irritation flickered across Thad's mind, but he gave no outward indication. 'Only when I have to be,' he said.

'I do wear a badge once in a while.'

'Well, that must mean you stay on the right side of the law.'

'Always,' Thad responded with careful emphasis. 'Do you always greet folks that way?'

Vic smiled around the match that he continually rolled from one side of his mouth to the other. 'Most of the time. Helps me size up a man if I keep him a little bit off guard. Come on in. The coffee pot's on. The missus will have some supper ready shortly.'

Thad hesitated. 'Well, maybe I'd oughta tell you why I'm here first.'

Vic's eyebrows rose. 'OK. Why don't you do that, then?'

Thad nodded, admiring the rancher's directness. 'I'm lookin' for a fella.'

'I figured that much. You think he's here?'

Thad nodded. 'One of the hands on the Twin T Bar told me a guy matching his description hired on here less'n a month ago.'

'Vince Long?'

Thad felt a sudden mixture of tension and excitement tighten his senses. 'That's the one. I'm surprised that he's using his own name.'

'It ain't the normal thing, if he's on the run. What's he done?'

'Killed a woman.'

'You don't say! One that needed killin'?'

Thad shook his head. 'No, not really. She was a whore, but she hadn't done nothin' to deserve gettin' a knife between her ribs.'

'I'll be wantin' to hear the story, but it looks like I got somethin' else to deal with first.'

Thad turned to look where the rancher's stare was fixed. Still a mile from the yard, something moved steadily in the fading light.

The rancher turned toward the bunkhouse and bellowed in a voice that could have probably been heard three miles upwind on a cloudy day. 'Frank! Willy! Got a problem.'

Almost instantly two cowboys erupted

94

from the bunkhouse door, guns in hand. They stopped short, staring at their boss for instruction. Vic pointed toward the faraway figure, still too small in the distance for Thad to make out anything other than it was something moving. 'Shaky's comin' in on foot. One of you saddle up and take an extra horse and go get him.'

Both hands looked toward where the rancher pointed. 'Is that Shaky?' one asked.

'It is if Vic says so,' the other rejoined as the two started for the barn. 'If Vic says he's got a cockle burr stuck in his left shirtsleeve, don't argue with him.'

Without breaking a smile Vic yelled after them, 'He don't, but he's some footsore, the way he's limpin'.'

Thad studied the distant figure. 'You got a good eye,' he admired.

'At a distance I do,' the rancher agreed. 'Can't hardly read no more, up close, but I can still count the fleas on a coyote's back at half a mile.'

They stood waiting, talking little, as

Frank rode from the yard at a swift trot, leading a saddled horse. As soon as they left the yard, the distant figure stopped. It was obvious he had no intention of walking another step, now that a horse was on its way.

When Frank got to him, Shaky stepped into the saddle and the pair trotted back to the ranch yard together. They rode directly to where Vic and Thad waited.

'What happened?' Vic asked as they approached.

Shaky turned and spit before he answered. There are few things more painful and awkward than having to walk any distance in a pair of riding boots. The high arch, the tall, under-slung heel, and the pointed toe are made for the needs of riding. They are torture to walk in.

Now, Shaky was on a horse again. His feet didn't hurt quite so much. Now he was more angry than in pain. Neither was he inclined to step down from the horse to talk to his boss. 'That dad-gummed no-account son-of-a-rabid-skunk you hired, that's what's wrong.'

'Long?'

'That's him. He stole my horse.'

'Why? What happened to his?'

'He's what happened to his horse. He shot 'im.'

By now every hand on the place was standing in a circle around Vic, Shaky and Thad. The announcement left all of them stunned, their mouths gaping open.

'Shot 'im?' Vic asked, his voice thundering incredulity. 'Why?'

Shaky turned and spit again, as if it were the only way he could adequately express his contempt and anger. He took a long breath. 'Well, we rode out this mornin' to check them cows over in Buck Canyon. We found 'em. 'Bout forty head. All doin' fine. Only one without a calf. Then we started back. A cottontail busted out of a clump o' sage brush. Long was ridin' that black stud o' his. It shied real hard, then it went an' blew up on him. Long wasn't expectin' it, and he wasn't ready. He got dumped. Landed right in a big ol' soap weed.'

'Never fails,' Vic commiserated. 'If there's a cactus or a soap weed in half a mile, that's where you always land.'

Shaky ignored the comment. 'He got up lookin' kinda funny like. His horse had stopped just as soon as Long bucked off. He was just standin' there, like a horse most usually does, head sorta down, just lookin' at him. Long just whipped out his gun an' shot 'im. Right between the eyes.'

Once again every jaw but Thad's dropped in astonishment. 'He shot that black stud he just got done breakin'?' Vic finally said.

Shaky spit again. 'Just as cold as ice. Didn't say a word. Then he turns and points his gun at me. 'Get off that horse,' he tells me, 'and start walkin'.''

After another stunned silence, Vic said, 'Well, at least he didn't shoot you.'

Shaky nodded. 'For once I'd kept my mouth shut, or he likely would've. I ain't never seen in a man's eyes what I seen in his. They was just flat an' cold as ice. It was almost exactly like lookin' into the eyes of a rattlesnake. I don't know what kept me from laughin' at him, sittin' there in that soapweed. If it'd been any of the other boys, I'da been hee-hawin' for sure. Sure am glad I didn't. I'da been just as dead as Midnight.'

'Well I'll be danged,' Vic breathed.

Nobody spoke for quite a while. It was Thad who finally broke the silence. 'What direction did he go?'

Shaky spit again. 'Danged if I know. He made me shuck my gun. Then he stood there with his gun pointed at me, not movin', like he was tryin' to decide whether to shoot me too, or just let me walk away. I just kept walkin', waitin' for a bullet in the back any minute. Just before I dropped over the hill out of his sight, I took a chance an' looked back. He was busy puttin' his own bedroll an' stuff on my horse. I wasn't about to stick around long enough to see where he was headin'. I made it to the bottom o' that draw and hid out in a plum thicket till I was sure he was good an' gone. Then I started ridin' shanks's mare back here.'

Vic turned to Thad. 'Well, I won't ask any more questions about why you're huntin' 'im. I pride myself in bein' a good judge o' men. I sure missed on him. I thought we'd hired us one o' the best horse wranglers I've ever seen.'

'He is a first rate horse wrangler,' the foreman interjected. 'Best I ever seen. I guess none of us had seen anythin' make him mad.'

Silence dominated the group for several minutes. Thad knew each man was thinking back over things he had said since Long had hired on, wondering how close he had come to triggering the man's lethal temper.

Finally, Vic said, 'Well, Thad, you're welcome to spend the night. I 'spect you'll be wantin' to head out at first light.'

Thad nodded. 'I'd appreciate that.'

He turned to Shaky. 'Would you mind takin' me out there so I can get a line on the direction of his tracks?'

'Happy to. Gotta go get my stuff anyway.'

'You said he took your saddle too?'

Shaky nodded. 'Looked like it. He either couldn't get his own out from the horse or didn't wanta try.'

'Is the one he left a good saddle?'

'Oh, yeah. It's actually a better saddle than mine. If he took my saddle, at least I got the best of that swap.'

The cowhand's eyes twinkled unexpectedly. ' 'Sides that, I was ridin' one o' the ranch horses, instead o' my own. I guess he done stole your horse, Vic.'

Every hand gathered around exploded in too-loud laughter that served to break the tension. Only Vic didn't smile. With a perfectly straight face he said, 'Careful, Shaky. I may take it outa your wages for not puttin' up more of a fight.'

Thad ignored the typical repartee, lost in wondering how many other things or people Vince Long would kill before he caught up with him. Or if he would feel a sense of responsibility, if it took him too long. It seemed wrong, somehow, that he had always felt some sense of responsibility for other men's crimes.

9

The trail was cold. Thad wasn't. Thad was steamed. Twice he had been close behind his elusive prey. Twice Long had slipped away and lengthened the distance between them. Thad wondered if the young fugitive was even aware he was tracking him.

He had been so close at the Flying V L. A few hours would have made the difference. But that few hours stretched the killer's lead to nearly a day, since he had to wait until daylight the next day to even begin trailing him.

His tracks were easy to follow at first. Then he had headed south and west, into rougher country, more hard soil and rocks than decent ground. He had eventually lost the trail, and now simply continued the same direction, hoping to spot whatever might attract the young man.

He followed a narrow trail that followed along the edge of a deep ravine. Above him, a low cliff did nothing to shade the trail, but it effectively prevented any ability to turn off the trail that direction. There were no tracks on the hard, bare rocks, which reflected the sun's heat. The trail topped a low rise and fell away. It continued, long and straight, for a good mile in front of him.

Just as he topped the rise and started down the other side, he thought he heard something behind him. He spun his horse and stood up in the stirrups. Nearly a half-mile behind him he spotted shadows moving on the further wall of the ravine.

His heart sank, then began beating wildly. Indians! He couldn't tell how many. It would almost certainly be either a hunting party or a war party. Too many to even think about confronting.

He turned back to look in the direction he had been heading. The trail stretched straight ahead much too far for him to have any hope of riding out of sight before the Indians topped the rise he had just ridden over.

He cast desperate looks around on all sides. Just ahead it looked like he might have a chance to ride to the bottom of the ravine. But what then? On the other hand, what choice did he have?

'C'mon, Tom,' he said. 'Let's give it a shot.'

The big gelding instantly sensed his master's fear. Barely hesitating, he began to follow the steeply sloping deer trail toward the bottom. His hoofs slipped and slid on the hard, slick rocks. He squatted his hindquarters close to the ground for balance, skidding as much as stepping, until they reached the narrow, flat bottom.

Thad cast swift, frightened glances both ways along the ravine. Back the way he had come, he could see a small area where the lip of the ravine formed an overhang. Beneath it, some long-ago sustained rush of floodwater had hollowed out a small cavity.

He urged the horse swiftly toward it. As he approached it, he leaped from the saddle. He led Tom up against the wall of rock, directly below the overhang. He pushed his hindquarters around, forcing him flat against the cool stone.

He and Tom had a lot of miles together behind them. Those miles had fostered a spirit of trust between horse and rider that minimized the horse's fear or resistance. When he had the horse as tightly against the bank as he could get him, he leaped back to place himself in front of him. Standing against the rock right in front of his horse's head, he grasped the bridle firmly. He spread his other hand across the horse's nose, to hold him from nickering a greeting to other passing horses. He held as still as possible, willing himself and his horse to be invisible.

A low murmur of talk drifted from the trail above. Then the first of the shadows appeared. Tom's ears lay back against his head, as he sensed the danger. Thad was afraid the gelding would bolt and run away up the ravine. If he did, the Indians would certainly come running to see where the horse's rider was. On foot and alone, he would have even less chance than mounted.

The bond of trust seemed to hold, second by second, minute by minute.

Shadows appeared on the far wall of the ravine. He could see feathers sprouting from headbands, points of spears jutting skyward, the shadows of bows and quivered arrows, and of a couple rifles. He silently counted as they passed above terrified man and horse. One. Two. Three. Four. Five. Six. Seven.

Someone in the group grunted suddenly. The group stopped, as if of a single volition. The shadows moved and distorted on the uneven wall of stone. The lead shadow bent low on his horse's neck, studying the ground. He pointed, saying something Thad couldn't understand.

The shadow moved back to an erect position on his horse. There was a brief discussion between members of the band. He sensed, rather than understood from their words, that they were discussing the fresh scuffs his descent had made down that deer trail. They seemed to ponder whether someone should descend to the floor of the ravine and investigate, or whether the scuffed and displaced rocks were caused by a passing deer.

Suddenly the group began to move again. Eight. Nine. Ten. Eleven. No more shadows. He stayed where he was, scarcely daring to breathe. He stood stock-still for fully ten minutes, just in case they had left someone behind. They seemed almost inhuman sometimes, in their ability to sense where others were hiding. He had heard endless stories on the subject. He didn't want to find out the hard way that the stories were accurate.

It was Tom who first became impatient with the wait. His keener senses knew full well the danger was gone. He jerked his head away from Thad's hand and snorted, pawing the ground.

Thad grabbed for his gun, waiting for someone to leap to the ravine floor beside him, tomahawk in hand. Nothing happened.

He breathed a huge sigh of relief. He moved out from under the overhang, and led Tom back to the deer trail they had clambered down. It was much harder going, getting back up. He urged, pulled, coaxed and led the horse up the steep incline. Then he stepped into the saddle and headed down the trail in the wake of the war party.

When the trail finally left the edge of the ravine the country began to flatten out somewhat. He picked a good point of vantage, and climbed to the top to survey the lay of the land ahead.

Careful to keep himself screened by trees and brush, he studied the route ahead of him carefully. To his right he saw the party of Indians, riding at a swift walk.

He turned his vision slowly toward the left, then stopped abruptly. A small wagon train, easily two miles away, was traveling in the same general direction as the war party. As he mentally measured the distances involved and the two directions of travel, it appeared that a meeting of the two was almost inevitable.

He clambered down from the top of the rimrock he had climbed to scan ahead. He sprang into the saddle. In the brief seconds after he had assessed the situation, he had mapped out what should be a relatively swift path. It would allow him to catch up with the slow moving wagon train from behind before they encountered the Indians. Maybe. If his horse didn't break a leg in a prairie-dog hole.

He didn't need any special coaxing to prod Tom into a swift, ground-eating lope. He bent low over the saddle horn, minimizing wind resistance as much as possible, striving to give the horse as few demands on its stamina as he could.

The ground here was better. It was softer, covered with good buffalo grass. That not only cushioned the horse's hoofs against the ground. It also muffled the sound of his running, so no errant breeze would carry its sound to the group of Indians.

It seemed to him that it took much too long, even so, before he cut across the wagon tracks. As if reading his rider's mind, Tom swung to go parallel with them.

Twenty minutes later he topped a low rise to see the wagon train stopped dead in its tracks.

His heart sank; he was certain he was too late. Then his reason told him there were no war cries. There were no shots being fired. The wagons were stopped for some other reason.

His galloping approach had attracted their attention, however. Two men with rifles flanked the last of the wagons, watching him warily.

He slid his horse to a stop and leaped from the saddle. 'There's a war party of Indians right over that ridge of hills, heading that way,' he announced. 'I don't know if they'll spot you or not, but you'd likely best be ready in case they do.'

Without questioning, one of the men whirled and ran for the front of the wagon train. The other said, 'How far away are they?'

Thad shook his head. 'I don't know, now. I just barely managed to keep 'em from spottin' me a ways back. Then I was scoutin' their whereabouts from a rimrock back yonder. I seen them goin' thataway, away from me, so that was good. Then I seen you folks, and it looked from there like you'd pertneart run together right about here.'

The lead wagons were already moving, circling around to form a defensive circle. Swift preparations without any hint of panic were taking place in and around all the wagons. Thad watched with approval, recognizing the skill with which the group was led.

He turned back to the man who had stayed with him. 'I was surprised to find you folks stopped.'

The man nodded. 'We was fixin' to send out a search party.'

'A search party?'

He nodded. 'One of our scouts come in an' said he'd found this here hollow that was plumb full of lamb's quarters and mushrooms that was good eatin'. One of the women went right off to start gatherin'. Several of the others got stuff together and went to help her. When they got there, Corky was gone.'

'Corky?'

'Coralee. We all call 'er Corky. Coralee Langdon. Her pa's the one that's leadin' this wagon train.'

'And she hasn't come back?'

'Nope. Now we're gonna have to wait till we find out what's happenin' with these Indians afore we can even look for 'er.'

Thad's mind was churning. Was it

possible Long had chanced upon her, out of sight and earshot of the others? Had she encountered a bear? What could have possibly have happened to her? Maybe she'd just twisted an ankle and couldn't walk. Should he go look for her? Should he stay here to help in case the Indians attacked?

He could never remember being swayed with uncertainty as he was in that moment. It suddenly angered him that he should be so indecisive.

He stepped into the saddle. 'Where's that hollow?'

'Quarter-mile back, 'bout a hundred yards south of our tracks.'

'I'll see what I can find,' he said as he spun Tom around and headed that direction.

The hollow was easy to find, but it would not have been visible from the trail. Lamb's quarters lifted their broad leaves in abundance. The mushrooms would be close to the ground, out of sight, but there was adequate moisture here to ensure their presence.

He rode along the edge of the trail side of the hollow until he spotted the matted grass where a set of tracks entered. He followed the path, easily visible from the saddle. Near the center of the patch, the vegetation was badly trampled in a fifteen-foot circle. Beyond the circle the bruised and crushed vegetation betrayed a single trail leading out of the hollow, toward a large copse of timber beyond.

He kicked Tom into a full gallop. At the edge of the hollow he realized he was following a trail left by a horse, not a person. Somebody had grabbed the woman, put her on a horse, and ridden away with her.

His first thought was another party of Indians. Then a hoofprint in a soft spot revealed that the horse was shod. He wasn't sure whether that was good news or bad.

Well into the copse of quivering aspens he stopped to study a flurry of tracks. It took him a minute to picture the activity, but it appeared that the woman had managed to leap off of the horse and run. The man had pursued her, first on horseback, then on foot. He followed their trail.

She had squirmed through a plum thicket, forcing him to leave his horse behind. Instead of trying to follow them, he followed the horse's trail in a straight line to beyond the plum thicket. He was rewarded with tracks again. They returned from the same direction in which she had fled. The tracks made it obvious that the man had caught her, but she was fighting him every step of the way.

The tracks led over a small bank, into another thicket of aspens. He followed on a run, leaving Tom to wait or trail behind him.

He was halfway to the aspens when he heard them. She had obviously managed to evade the man once again, for a long while. Her voice was defiant, promising all kinds of drastic alterations of his physique. His was angry, menacing. The sound of a fist against flesh abruptly stopped her tirade against him.

Through the trees Thad could make out the man bending over a supine woman, tearing at her clothing. In his own haste he stepped on a fallen branch. It snapped with a report almost as loud as a gunshot.

A gunshot would have had hardly more dramatic effect than the snap of the twig. The man instantly wheeled and bolted. The gun in Thad's hand, which he didn't even remember drawing, roared impossibly loud in the quiet of the aspen grove. Bark erupted from a tree trunk inches from the man's face, showering him with sharp fragments. He yelped and dived to the side, ducking and dodging out of sight. Almost immediately the sound of a fleeing horse crashing through the brush and trees attested to his departure.

Once again Thad was torn with indecision. Should he sprint back to Tom and pursue? Should he see to the woman? She chose that moment to moan and stir, obviously returning to consciousness. That made the decision for him.

He rushed to her, kneeling beside her. He moved her torn blouse the better to cover her. He looked at her rapidly swelling face. She had been slugged in a nearly identical manner to Millie, the saloon girl. He knew with absolute certainty who her assailant had been. He also knew the trail would once again be cold by the time he returned to it.

The woman moaned. Her eyes fluttered open. She jerked erect, eyes wide with fright and anger. He backed away, holding both hands out in front of himself. 'It's OK, ma'am. Corky, ain't it?'

She blinked in confusion. Her eyes cast about frantically for a moment, then came back to dwell on him. 'Who . . . where . . . is he gone?'

'I scared him off, ma'am. I didn't have a clear shot, or I'd have dropped him where he stood.'

'You . . . you know him?'

'I know too much about him. I been trailing 'im for quite a ways.'

'What . . . who are you?'

'The name's Thad Palmer, ma'am.'

'How did you know my name?'

'Fella at your wagon train told me.'

She was clearly regaining her faculties. 'Where are the others?'

'They got the wagons circled. I spotted a war party that might happen to run into 'em, so they're ready just in case.'

A sudden thought made him jerk his head up, and he looked quickly in all directions. He listened intently.

'What is it?' she demanded, sensing his alarm, her own fear rising in response.

'Just hopin' the shot I fired at that guy didn't reach the war party. I wouldn't want 'em headin' this way.'

She scrambled to her feet. Unaware of the degree to which Long had ripped her blouse, she made no immediate effort to cover herself. Thad quickly turned his back. 'You'd best see if you can fix that shirt, ma'am. Then we'll head back.'

She squealed with sudden embarrassment as she realized why he had so suddenly turned his back. Then she giggled. She fumbled with the abused cloth, finding two buttons that would still function adequately to keep her covered. 'You can turn back around now,' she announced. 'How do we get out of here?'

In answer he lifted his head and whistled sharply. In seconds he was rewarded with the cautious steps of his horse working his way through the trees to them. His head was held to one side, to avoid stepping on the dragging reins.

'Oh, my!' Corky enthused, with a good humor belying her circumstances. 'The knight in shining armor even has a horse that comes to the rescue when summoned.'

'Yeah, he's my kinda horse,' Thad responded. 'He'll do most anything for a damsel in distress.'

He liked the sound of her giggle. He motioned to the horse. 'Go ahead and get on. I'll walk.'

'Won't he ride double?'

'Well, yeah, I 'spect he would.'

'Then go ahead and get on. I'll climb on behind you.'

He hesitated the briefest moment, then stepped into the saddle. He kicked his foot free of the stirrup. She lifted her foot into it, grabbed the saddle horn, and swung lightly into the saddle behind him. As she did, the motion placed her arm around him. He liked the thrill that radiated through him at the touch.

She made no effort to remove the arm. She simply kicked the stirrup loose, then took hold of his waist on both sides. He tried to ignore the presence of her hands there as Tom worked his way through the trees, back to the hollow, across it to the trail, then to the wagon train.

10

'Did the war party show up?'

'Yup. They showed up along that hill. They was about a quarter mile away. They looked us over real good. They seen we was all circled an' ready for 'em. I guess they decided we was gonna be more'n that many of 'em could handle, so they rode off.'

'Are you sure they rode off?'

'Yup. We sent the scouts to make sure. They're three miles off an' still goin' t'other way.'

'Well, I guess it was good you were ready.'

'We got you to thank for that. Looks like we got you to thank for bringin' Corky back, too. You OK, Corky?'

In fact, she seemed to be OK again. Less than halfway between where he had rescued her and the wagon train, Coralee had lost her show of bravado.

The elation of being rescued was slowly washed away by the residue of trauma, and by recognition of what a close call she had experienced.

Thad had felt it happening, and had known of nothing to do about it, so he did nothing. Corky's hands, which had started the ride resting lightly on the sides of his waist, slowly crept upward and around him. As she allowed herself to think about the horror she had so narrowly escaped, thoughts of what might have happened seeped through her awareness. She began to tremble. As she trembled, she clutched ever more tightly to her rescuer, pressing close against him.

Then the tears came. He felt, rather than heard, as she fought to weep silently. Her tears began to soak the back of his shirt. Then her sobs became audible. Great racking sobs, that shook her whole body, making her grip him even tighter.

He slowed his horse, deliberately taking much longer than necessary to make it back to the wagon train. He somehow thought she needed the time.

Her sobs slowly abated, then stopped. He felt her take a deep, ragged breath. She released her hold on him. Using a sleeve of her torn blouse, she mopped the tears from her face. Then, in a move typical of men everywhere, but never seen among women, she turned her head, held one nostril shut with a finger, and blew her nose explosively into the air. Then she turned her head the other way and cleared the other nostril in the same manner.

'I'm OK now,' she had told him.

He took her at her word and continued toward the wagon train.

★   ★   ★

Now she answered the young man to whom Thad was talking. 'I'm fine, Ted. Thad found us before that guy had a chance to do anything much.'

'What guy?' Ted demanded instantly.

'A guy I been huntin',' Thad explained.

'He spotted her pickin' greens, and grabbed her.'

Ted looked back and forth between Thad and Corky several times. 'Did you get 'im?' he asked then.

Thad shook his head. 'Came close, but he got away.'

Ted looked at Corky again. 'You'd best get to your family's wagon,' he advised. 'Your folks are worried sick about you.'

With no further talk, Thad lifted the reins, guiding Tom to the wagon that Corky pointed out. As they approached, her mother ran forward. 'Oh, Corky! Are you OK?'

'I'm fine now, Mother,' Corky responded.

In spite of her spoken assurance, she bailed off the horse and into her mother's embrace. Her father was beside them, as if suddenly spirited there from some unseen place.

'You OK, Corky?' was his first question as well.

'I'm going to have a huge black eye, but I'm fine,' she assured him, her voice muffled from her face being buried in her mother's shoulder. 'Thad found us and chased the guy off and brought me back.'

She jerked away from her mother. 'Oh, Mother, Pa, this is Thad Palmer. He tracked us from where that guy grabbed me, and chased him off. Then he brought me home, so can I keep him?'

Her parents seemed not at all surprised by the seemingly inappropriate humor. With a straight face her father said, 'Well, I don't know. Is he house-broke?'

'I'm not sure, but he talks well.'

'You two stop it!' her mother demanded. Her voice sounded exasperated, but her eyes were twinkling. She stepped forward and held out her hand. 'I'm Cora Langdon. I apologize for those two. You never know what either one of them is going to say next. Thank you for rescuing our daughter. We owe you a huge debt for that.'

Reaching down from the saddle,

Thad returned the strong grip of her hand. 'Happy to meet you, ma'am.'

'I'm not a 'ma'am',' she insisted at once. 'I'm just Cora.'

'And I'm Walt,' her father said, stepping forward and extending his own hand. 'I'm the patsy these two keep beaten into silent submission.'

'Glad to meet you.' Thad grinned as he returned that handshake as well.

'Well, get down and take care of your horse,' Walt ordered. 'You'll be stayin' for supper, of course. You'd just as well bed down with the bunch here too. Mornin' will be time enough to head out after that guy you're trailin'. You did say that's the guy that grabbed my girl, didn't you?'

The thought of spending the night hadn't occurred to Thad, but he couldn't think of a reason to refuse. He was more intrigued about Walt already knowing why he was here, and that Corky's abductor was the prey he was hunting. Clearly, there was more to this guy than met the eye.

'I'd be obliged,' was all he said as he dismounted and began to see to his horse.

A group of women, this time with an armed escort, returned to the hollow to harvest a generous amount of the greens and mushrooms. They were shared all around, and became a part of most of the *entrées du jour*, cooked over a dozen campfires within the circle of wagons.

What followed was easily the most enjoyable evening Thad could remember spending. Ever. Even aside from Corky's presence. The entire party, except for the carefully placed sentries, gathered together for the evening meal. Each family prepared their own, for the most part, but then they shared with one another freely.

During the meal conversation was light and convivial. Even when things were discussed that might have been controversial, they were discussed with a mutual respect that he thought rare.

Rarer still was the whole group's

acceptance of him as an equal. He had never been allowed to be that much a part of 'polite society'. He was a gun-fighter. A hired killer. That was all most people needed to know to shun him as if he were a leper.

It was that open acceptance that made the meal the finest of his life, even though he couldn't remember what he'd eaten. It didn't hurt a thing, either, that Corky sat on the ground near him the entire time. She had changed and cleaned up after their return, then went about helping with the routine of cooking and cleaning up, as if nothing had happened to her. He found himself chatting more easily with her than he could remember doing with any woman. Or man either, for that matter.

Supper was no more than finished when a fiddle, a guitar and a mouth harp appeared. The musically talented trio entertained, played accompaniment for songs someone suggested they should all sing, and for an occasional couple who decided to do a little impromptu dancing.

At a lull in the music, Walt said, 'I 'spect we'd best be turnin' in. We need to make up a little lost time tomorrow. We'll be headin' out about an hour earlier than usual.'

The others responded by immediately rising to retire to their own wagons. The evening social time was over.

Thad self-consciously drifted to the Langdons' wagon, and visited a while longer. His inquiry revealed the location of their destination. A wide valley, about thirty miles beyond where they were now, had been selected as a site for a new community they intended to found. It had good water, plentiful grass, good timber, and everything needed to establish farms and ranches. It was also near enough to other settled areas to have access to supplies, and the company of other settlers. It sounded ideal.

Stumbling for words and feeling awkward, he finally turned to Corky.

'Ma'am, when you get there, and when I get this here business I'm committed to taken care of, would you mind if I sorta moseyed around that way, and, uh . . . I mean, uh, called on you?'

Corky giggled. Even in the rapidly darkening twilight he could see her eyes dance. 'Only if you promise to never, ever call me 'ma'am' again.'

The best Thad could do was mumble, 'Thanks,' as he hurried to where he had left his bedroll. He spent a great deal more time thinking about what that might lead to, as he lay in his blankets watching the myriad stars. They seemed to shine a lot brighter than he could remember.

11

A solid week of frustration had left Thad Palmer tired, irritable and discouraged. He had hoped to pick up Long's trail immediately, chase him to ground, then hurry to a certain valley south and west.

Instead he had lost Long's trail several times. Finding it again took time. It took far too much time to cross the rough, almost entirely unpopulated area. Now the trail led into a more settled region. Dozens of trails intersected and branched off, with myriad tracks that made it nearly impossible to pick out those left by the fugitive.

Now he had been forced to rely on questioning nearly everyone he ran across. Most of the time that proved futile. Enough times it yielded adequate results to keep him close to his quarry, but never close enough to confront him.

He had concluded from some of those conversations that Vince was heading in the general direction of Clarkstown. Indications were that it served as something of a hub for an area of ranches and homesteads. He made the decision to ride directly there, in hopes the guess was accurate.

As he passed through an area of hardwood timber in a broad valley, he heard voices from off to his right. He reined in his horse, listening intently. He was too far away to make out the words, but one voice in particular was high, strident, clearly fraught with terror.

He reined Tom off the trail and headed slowly, cautiously, toward the voices.

He had worked his way through 300 yards of trees when he approached a wide clearing. Half a dozen men sat their horses, staring straight away from him.

The object of their hostile stares was a young man on the shy side of twenty. He was also mounted, but his hands were tied behind him. A noose around his neck ran to a branch above him, then down to where it was secured around the base of the tree.

'I swear to God,' the young man was saying, 'I didn't do it. I wouldn't never do anything like that. I wasn't even over on that side of the valley. You gotta listen to me!'

'Abbey give us a description,' one of the men growled. 'You fit the description to a T.'

'But I don't even know her.'

'She didn't know you neither. That's why she couldn't tell us your name.'

'But it wasn't me!'

'We caught you ridin' away.'

'Not from her, I wasn't. I'd just been sent over to Waltman's to take back a horse my boss had borrowed. I was on the way back to the ranch.'

'You was headin' straight away from where it happened. You was in a hurry. You fit the description. I don't know nobody in the valley that it fits better.'

'But it wasn't me, I'm telling you. On

my mother's grave, I swear it. So help me God, it wasn't me.'

Another man spoke up. 'We've palavered long enough. Let's get it done.'

He urged his horse forward, took off his hat, and prepared to swat the young man's horse on the rump.

'You boys sure you got the right guy?'

Thad's voice cut across the clearing like a bolt of lightning. Its effect was just as strong. Every man whirled in the saddle to face the unexpected intrusion.

The young man about to be a lynching victim had the strongest reaction. The despairing panic in his eyes turned to sudden, desperate hope. Tears began to stream down his face. 'Oh, mister! Don't let 'em do this to me. I ain't done nothin' wrong. Honest! Especially that there. I wouldn't never do that there to nobody.'

The group of men looked uneasily back and forth between their fellows. Each one's eyes kept darting to the rifle that Thad held casually across his legs, pointed in their general direction. That his hand was gripping the stock, his finger on the trigger, was not lost to any of them.

'Exactly what is it this fella's bein' hung for?' he asked.

The group of men all looked at one another, each obviously hoping someone else would explain their actions to this interloper. Finally one of them, the one that had been a second away from sending the horse out from under the victim, spoke. 'He grabbed a girl and drug her off into the brush and forced himself on her. Any man that'd rape a woman deserves to hang, and that's what we're fixin' to do. It ain't any of your business, whoever you are.'

'How sure are you that he did it?'

'Sure enough.'

'Sure enough don't seem all too sure, to me. What happens if she looks at this guy after he's hung and dead, and says, 'No, that's not the guy'?'

Half a dozen men squirmed uneasily in their saddles. One of them reached up to scratch his head, just behind his right ear. He eyed the speaker of his group expectantly, awaiting the answer.

'He's the guy,' the other argued. 'Why else would he be runnin' away like that?'

Thad carefully kept his voice calm, as friendly as he could manage. 'Well, did you check out his story about returnin' a horse?'

Again the group cast uneasy glances back and forth. Nobody answered.

Thad pressed the issue. 'This girl that was raped — was she a young girl?'

'Barely sixteen.'

'Was she bloodied up any?'

All the men turned as one to look at one of their group. He nodded. From his expression, Thad deduced that the girl was either his daughter or well known to him. 'She was hurt pretty bad. He was plumb brutal.'

Thad nodded. 'Did you find any traces of blood on this guy? He don't look to me like someone that's changed clothes for a week or two.'

The would-be victim looked quickly down at his own clothes, clearly wondering if his less than fastidious habits might actually be his salvation.

'I didn't even think o' that,' one of the men said. 'He should have, all right, if it was him.'

'He coulda took his clothes off afore he did it.'

'Then he'd have blood on him. Did you check?'

'He coulda warshed.'

'He don't look like he's done much o' that lately, either.'

Again there was a long pause with no response.

Thad decided to play his best hunch. 'I'll tell you boys somethin' else you might wanta think about. I been several weeks already trackin' a woman-killer. He's just about the same size and age as the young man over there. Just over a week ago, he grabbed a young lady from a wagon train that had gone off out of sight of the others. He dragged her into a clump of timber, and was

138

fixin' to do to her just what you're describing happened to that girl. I got there quick enough to run him off, but I missed him and he got away.'

'You think it was him?' one of the men asked, as if asking whether he thought it might have been the Easter bunny.

'Don't know,' Thad responded. 'Sounds like his style, though.'

He locked gazes with the man who had knowledge of the girl's condition. 'One of this guy's favorite things to do is to slug a woman, right there.'

He put a fist against his face, just beside the eye. 'He hits 'em hard enough to pertneart knock 'em out, so they can't resist, but so they'll be awake enough to know what he's doin' to 'em. Does that ring a bell?'

The man stared back at Thad as if he had just done some amazing feat of sorcery. 'That there's just exactly what he done, all right,' he admitted. 'At least that's just exactly the way she described it.'

From the expressions, Thad was

almost certain the mob mentality had been breached, and he had won the day. His biggest concern now was the one so eager to slap the horse and watch the young man do a death dance on the end of the rope. He could still act in an instant, and it would be difficult to save him at that point.

They were interrupted by sounds of a horse crashing through the trees and brush. Accompanying the snapping branches and violated brush was an urgent voice calling, 'Cal! Where you at, Cal?'

The nearly lynched young man's eyes brightened. 'Over here, Wes!'

In seconds another young man burst into the glen. He was about Cal's age, but blockier built. His garb identified him immediately as another cowboy. 'Hey,' Wes yelled as he entered the scene, 'I heard what was goin' on. Someone told me where you was headin' with Cal. Listen! Cal didn't do it. Cal was with the whole crew on the Box D last night, when they said that happened. It couldn'ta been him.'

The rape victim's father, as Thad had finally decided, instantly demanded, 'Were you there?'

'Yeah. Yeah, we was all in the bunkhouse last night. You can ask any hand on the Box D. They'll tell you. It was sunup today when he left to take a horse back to Waltman's. He was supposed to hurry some, 'cause we was movin' cows and needed every hand. When he didn't come back right away, I got worried somethin' had happened to 'im, so I come lookin'. That's when someone told me you thought he'd raped someone last night early. Well, I knowed right off that couldn'ta possibly been Cal, 'cause he was with the rest of us all night.'

Looking decidedly disappointed, the man who most worried Thad put his hat back on. He rode up beside Cal and lifted the noose off his neck. Flipping the noose back over the branch, he let the rope fall to the ground. He pulled a knife from his belt and severed the rope holding the young man's hands tied securely behind him.

Cal rubbed his wrists, looking around at the circle of faces staring at him. He looked up at the limb of the tree above him. Then he looked at the tangle of rope on the ground. Abruptly he dived from the saddle, bent over and began throwing up.

Thad shoved his rifle into the saddle scabbard and nudged his horse over to the young girl's father. Before he could say anything, the man said, 'I want to thank you, stranger, whoever you are. You kept us from makin' a terrible mistake here today.'

Ignoring that, Thad said, 'Can you show me where it happened? If I get right on this guy's tracks, I might have a chance to catch up with him.'

The man nodded mutely. He turned his horse and began to pick his way toward the road, with Thad close behind.

12

Vince Long was furious. It never occurred to him to be angry with himself. It was the girl that was the problem.

'How come women are all like that?' he demanded of the stolen horse he was riding. 'They smile at you. They give you that look. They gotta know there ain't no man alive what ain't turned on by that look. Then they start playin' games.'

He rode his horse into a stream. He dismounted in the ice-cold water. He pulled off his boots and socks, then stripped off his pants. He looked at his long underwear, and realized he needed to remove it as well.

He angrily jerked off his shirt, then shed the underwear. Pants and underwear were both badly bloodstained. Shivering in the icy water, he washed himself and his clothes. He did his best to remove all traces of blood. Then he shrugged back into his wet clothes.

He tried to pull his boots on, but struggled to get the sodden footwear to slip on.

Swearing profusely, he sat down in the frigid stream so he could raise his leg and use both hands to pull on the boot straps. As he did, the freezing water that filled the boot ran down his leg. He released another string of profanities. Pulling hard he managed to get first one, then the other boot on.

He got back on his horse and kicked the animal far harder than necessary to cross the stream the rest of the way, and continue onward.

'Gonna catch my death,' he muttered. He shivered, reaching behind himself for his slicker. 'Prob'ly die o' pneumonia, all on account o' that stupid girl.'

The sun and the slicker's presence slowly began to warm him enough for his violent shivering to subside. As it did, his mood began to lighten.

'Sure showed her what a real man's like, though, I did. She'll know better'n to go battin' them big ol' eyelashes at somebody after this.'

He actually laughed, relishing his reliving of what the girl would relive with horror endlessly.

The more he thought about her devastation, the abject dejection of her distorted face when he had left her lying in the grass, the lighter his mood became.

'Had it comin', that's for sure,' he reassured himself.

He laughed suddenly. 'That idiot that pertneart shot me back yonder didn't get here quick enough this time. He ain't gonna, neither. I bet he wasn't even from the wagon train. Betcha a double eagle he's been on my trail ever since I stuck that whore in Lone Tree.'

He went on muttering to himself for a while. Then he began to sing. He sang to himself for a long while, before he fell into another long silence.

'Had it comin', she did,' he said aloud. He didn't need to explain to himself which 'she' he was referring to.

As if some random thought had abruptly intruded into whatever else he was thinking of, his head jerked up. 'I gotta get me some money. I ain't had a chance to hole up anywheres long enough to earn any wages.'

That was on his mind as he rode slowly into Dry Creek late in the afternoon. He put his horse up in the livery barn, careful to rub him down and give him a carefully measured amount of oats. Then he wandered up the street to the town's sole café. He ate a tough steak with a big mound of fried potatoes, and paid for it with what was nearly the last of his money.

He had enough left for a couple drinks, at least.

He strolled next door to the saloon, ordered a beer, and sipped it slowly. Little by little, the attention of the saloon's patrons focused on a table near the center. A game of poker was in

146

progress in which the stakes had steadily increased. Five men were involved. Four of them evidently had a good hand at the same time. Each was confident his hand was better than what the others evidently thought was a winning hand. The fifth player had laid down his cards early on, knowing his hand had no chance to beat four good hands.

One of the four appeared to be a gambler, or at least something far different from the rest. The other four were all cattlemen or cowboys. Cattlemen, almost certainly, by the size of the pot. Not many cowboys could save money long enough to have that kind of a stake.

'Well, I guess I'm called,' one of the cattlemen acknowledged. He laid down his cards. 'I got a straight. Jack high.'

The man next on his left smiled. 'I was hopin' that's what you was relyin' on, Chet.' He laid down his own hand. 'I got a flush. Ten high.'

The man to the other side of the first

said, 'Well, I guess I got you both beat. I went and got myself a full house.'

He laid the cards on the table and reached for the pile.

The gambler said, 'Not too quick, my friend. I do believe my four lovely ladies are pretty enough to beat a full house.'

He laid a hand with four queens on the table. Three cattlemen expelled the same obscene word in the same breath.

'Don't that beat all?' one of them expostulated. 'Four hands like that in the same hand. Who'da thought it?'

The gambler raked in the pot, his face impassive. 'Lady Luck does like to play games with us,' he said. 'I usually end up on the losing end of those kinds of hands.'

The others pushed back from the table and headed for the bar to commiserate with each other. The gambler carefully placed the folding money in one part of a money belt, and the gold and silver coins in another. He buckled it under his shirt, adjusted his jacket over it, and headed for the door.

None of the saloon's patrons had noticed Vince Long slip out the door just moments ahead of him.

The gambler stopped in front of the door of the saloon. He took in a deep breath of the night air. It had been the best night he'd had in a long while. He was due. His luck hadn't been running very good for a while. It was probably time to catch a stage to a different town, before anyone started wondering how four great hands would show up in the same hand, when it was his turn to deal. He started down the board sidewalk toward the hotel.

He was just even with the space between the saloon and the store next to it, when a searing pain slammed into his back and side. The breath seemed to be driven from his lungs.

He turned to find the source, but was jerked off his feet, into the deep shadows between the buildings. He fought to orient himself. He felt dizzy. No, it was more like feeling faint. It was a lot like drifting off to sleep, but he couldn't make himself wake up. Darkness seemed somehow to be settling over him, enveloping him. Then there was nothing.

Vince carefully wiped his knife blade on the sleeve of the gambler's jacket. Then he ripped the money belt from around his waist. Fastening it around his own middle, he tucked his shirt in and headed for the livery barn at a swift walk. Ten minutes later he was headed out of town at a swift trot.

13

The trail was fresh. It was easier to follow. Fleetingly, Thad wondered if Vince had figured out he was being pursued when he had shot at him.

He shook his head. 'Woulda more likely been someone from the wagon train, lookin' for Corky,' he murmured, dismissing the idea. 'He's got no way to know I been hired to chase him down.'

He crossed a small stream, then stopped and studied the trail carefully. 'He's at least three hours ahead of me,' he muttered. 'His horse woulda dripped quite a bit o' water comin' outa that stream. It's plumb dried up.'

He lifted his gaze to the road ahead. 'Likely headin' wherever this road takes him, for the time being,' he surmised. 'Just as well try to make up a little time.'

He nudged Tom into a swift trot. At

least Long was traveling the right direction. Every mile he traveled this direction brought him back closer to the valley where the Langdons' party planned to settle. The thought of getting back to where he could spend some time with Corky lightened his mood and made the miles fall away behind him.

The sun was already relinquishing the land to the darkness that ever pursued it when Thad spotted a town ahead. He barely had light enough to read 'Dry Creek' on the carefully painted sign that announced its identity.

'I wonder how they ever got 'e's in 'Crick', anyway,' he asked his horse as they eased to a walk. 'That don't even make sense.'

The horse seemed to instinctively know where the livery barn was. Maybe he could hear other horses in the corral behind it, or in the stalls. Maybe he could smell the hay or the oats. Maybe he sensed something in his rider that indicated direction. Whatever it was, he trotted unerringly to that establishment. Thad turned him over to the hostler with instructions, shouldered his bedroll, and headed for the hotel.

He ate a hot supper in the hotel's dining room and retired to his room. He pondered the odds of whether his quarry was in town, or had merely passed through. Close behind him as he knew himself to be, it seemed extremely likely he was in town. That meant he'd be in the only saloon he'd noticed riding in.

He checked his gun, carefully cleaning the trail dust from it, reloaded it, and dropped it into its holster. He left the hotel, walking diagonally across the street.

He was barely into the street when someone on the other side burst out of a dark space next to the saloon and darted inside. In seconds several men followed him back out, all hurrying in the direction from which the man had come.

A few steps behind them, another came out carrying a lantern.

He hurried across the street, alarm bells ringing in his head. By the time he got there, two men were bending over a prone figure in the darkness. The others stood in a half-circle, watching.

The lantern cast its yellow glow on the form of a well-dressed, but clearly dead, man.

'It's the gambler,' one of the men announced.

'Deader'n a doornail,' a second affirmed.

'Money belt's gone.'

'Stabbed him, looks like. Right in the back.'

The first speaker addressed the bartender, who had brought the lantern. 'Did you see anyone leave right after he did?'

The bartender shook his head, as if anyone could see him do so in the darkness. 'No,' he said, thinking hard. 'The only one that left right about then was that young stranger. He left right ahead of him.'

'After the gambler had won that big pot?'

'Yeah, come to think of it, it was right shortly after. Right after Chance put all his money in that money belt he always wears.'

'So he saw him do that?'

The bartender's voice was thoughtful, but emanated a high degree of certainty. 'Yeah, I'm pretty sure he did. Sure could have, anyway.'

A third voice, that hadn't yet spoken, gave voice to a sudden thought. 'The livery barn! Two to one he's gettin' his horse to light out.'

The group instantly abandoned the company of the dead in pursuit of the living. They ran, Thad among them, to the livery barn. 'Hey Nick!' one of them hollered as they approached.

The hostler appeared at once. 'What's goin' on?'

'Where's that stranger?'

'Did that young cowpoke come and get his horse?'

'Is he still here?'

'Where is he?'

Everybody spouting questions at once lent an air of excitement, but it made it difficult to understand any of them. 'What?' Nick asked.

Eventually they simmered down enough to let one man speak. 'Did a young cowpoke have his horse put up here?'

'Yeah, he did. He's gone now, though.'

'When did he leave?'

'Oh, good hour ago. About fifteen, twenty minutes after that fella there brung his horse in.'

Several glanced at Thad then back to the hostler.

'What way did he go?'

'He lit out off thataway,' he said, pointing down the waterless valley from which the town obviously drew its name. 'I thought it was kinda odd he didn't take the road, but didn't think a whole lot about it. Why?'

'He stabbed and robbed that gambler that's been hangin' around town the past couple weeks.'

'You don't say! Kill him?'

'Yeah, he's dead.'

'You don't say!'

Silence enveloped the group as they stared into the darkness the direction the hostler had pointed. Finally one of them said, 'Not much sense tearin' out after him in the dark.'

Thad spoke for the first time. 'I'll be on his trail at first light,' he said. 'I've been trailing him a long way. I got this close. I'll catch up to him.'

'Who're you?'

'Name's Thad Palmer. I've been following him clear from Lone Tree.'

'That a pretty far piece. Must be a bad apple.'

'Real bad.'

'Who is he?'

'He's a man in bad need of hanging. His name's Vince Long. He's left a trail of dead folks all the way. Women mostly.'

'Woman killer?'

'And worse.'

'Well, I hope you catch up to him.'

'I will. Sooner or later.'

The group began to drift away, carrying on low conversations between them. Most of them were headed back to the saloon.

14

The first rays of the sun missed Dry Creek. They were aimed too high, bathing the tops of the nearby mountains in light instead. Even so, they spilled enough from the edges of the beams of sunlight to illuminate the earth. Those splashes of errant light were oblique enough to cast shadows from the slightest of the ground's aberrations. That made Vince's tracks easier to follow than they would be, even in the midday sun.

Thad was taking full advantage of that detail. He was in the saddle and waiting, when those first spillovers of sunlight enabled him to continue his quest. He followed the trail at the swift trot his horse was capable of for long periods.

'Gotta find a chance to let him rest a day or two pretty quick, though,' Thad told himself. 'He's runnin' on heart.'

He knew Long wouldn't likely keep going long in the darkness. It had been a moonless night, and riding in strange country in the dark was always an iffy business. He guessed the fugitive would put enough distance between himself and the town to feel secure, then he'd bed down until daylight.

That meant he should just now be stirring. He might find a vantage point to watch his backtrail, to see if the town gathered a posse and launched a pursuit. Thad thought it unlikely. The gamblers who drifted through from time to time were never highly regarded. Usually they were barely tolerated. Most considered them to be a form of parasite that was just there, like ticks and fleas. Nobody cared where they came from. Nobody cared where they went when they left. You might win some money off of one of them if you got lucky. That slim chance was enough for them to be tolerated. Nothing more.

That made it unlikely that the town

would more than scarcely remember him by the time a full day had passed. It would end up being the undertaker's sole responsibility to lay him to rest in the small cemetery on top of the rocky knoll. The town parson, if there was one, might or might not say a few words that only God would hear.

Vince surely knew that. That, and the abundance of money that was apparently in the big pot he had won, made him the perfect target, at the perfect time. Easy money. Little risk.

No, Thad decided, it was unlikely he would even worry about pursuit. Now that he had money, he wouldn't be heading anywhere that promised the likelihood of a job. He would more likely be looking for a place with saloons and whores whom he could abuse.

By midday Thad was growing increasingly uneasy. Vince's path was taking him south and west again. They couldn't be more than a half day's ride from the valley where Corky and the promise of everything he'd dreamed about since meeting her awaited. He had to catch up with the demented deviant before he had opportunity to make another attempt on Corky. He picked up the pace of his pursuit.

He topped a long ridge and reined in abruptly. Below him spread the most beautiful valley he had ever seen. It stretched probably twenty miles from side to side. Snow-capped mountains rimmed it in the distance, clearly visible in the high, dry, clear air. At the center a river ran in twists and oxbows, frequently stemmed and slowed by beaver dams and marshy areas. Verdant grass rippled in the late afternoon breeze.

Near the valley's center he could see activity. He could make out a cluster of tents, and some buildings in the initial stages of construction. Cattle and horses grazed nearby.

That had to be them! Corky was somewhere within the range of his sight! He had to get down there as quickly as possible. He told himself it was to warn them of Vince's presence in the valley. Deep down he knew it had more to do with being close to Corky.

He lifted his reins and started down a wide trail. It had been worn over centuries by the countless hoofs of deer, elk, moose, and the predators that continually stalked them.

He passed through a thick stand of spruce and northern pines, where the trail faded as a dozen lesser trails led out from it.

He emerged into sunlight again, bent on reaching the budding settlement. His heart was already racing.

Suddenly, lights exploded in his brain.

He never heard the report of the rifle that echoed off the sides of the valley. He never felt himself flop from the saddle. He didn't feel himself sprawl on the deep grass.

Tom, his faithful horse, stopped instantly. The reins, dropped by a hand no longer there, trailed on the ground.

He turned his head and looked at his master, motionless on the ground. He snorted at the smell of blood coming from his head, making a dark stain on the ground. He tossed his head, and waited, for the master who would not get up and mount him again.

15

Three men, felling trees at the edge of a thick stand of timber, stopped their axes in mid-swing.

'Wonder who that is?' one of them said.

'Did somebody go out huntin' today?'

'Not that I know of.'

'It was a rifle.'

'Uh huh.'

'Just one shot.'

'Uh huh.'

Silence for half a minute. Then, 'Whatd'ya think?'

'Wouldn't hurt to check it out.'

The other two nodded agreement. All three walked over to where their gunbelts hung on a broken branch of a cedar. They buckled them on, then began to walk together toward the sound they had all heard.

They climbed steadily for fifteen minutes. Then they heard the retreating hoofbeats of a horse.

'Did you see 'im?'

'Just caught a glimpse through the trees.'

'Could you see who it was?'

'Naw. Just saw the flash of motion.'

'Whoever it was spotted us.'

'Uh huh.'

'Wasn't just huntin', or he wouldn'ta took off like that.'

'Uh huh.'

Their pace picked up perceptibly. Five minutes later a horse nickered. They all stopped as if the sound had been a rope stretched across their path. They stood stock still, listening intently.

'Came from over there.'

'Uh huh.'

As one they drew their pistols and moved forward cautiously.

'I see 'im!' one of them whispered loudly.

'Where?'

'Right through there.'

'Oh, yeah. I see him.'

'Dead?'

'Looks it.'

The tableau became apparent to all of them at once. Somebody had been killed, shot from ambush. The killer had been headed down into the valley, but had spotted them and reversed course. Now he was gone, and they were left with a dead man to tend to.

They walked swiftly to where he lay. His horse stood half a dozen paces away, nervously tossing his head, but standing his ground.

'Hey! I know that horse.'

'You do?'

'Yeah. It's that gunfighter's. The one who found Corky and brung her back.'

'I think you're right. Is that the guy?'

'Sure looks like it. Lotta blood on his face, but I think that's him.'

'Looks like whoever shot 'im got 'im right between the eyes.'

'Close to it, anyway.'

They knelt beside Thad. One of them, for some reason he couldn't understand, pulled off his neckerchief. He wiped away some of the blood that covered Thad's face.

An odd expression crossed his face. He held a hand next to Thad's nose. 'Hey! He's breathin'! He's still alive!'

'With a hole like that in his head?'

A second man laid a hand on his chest. 'He is! His heart's beatin'.'

'Ain't gonna be for long. A man don't survive gettin' shot between the eyes.'

'Well, it's a little high.'

'Hard to tell with all that blood.'

'So what're we gonna do?'

Silence. Then, 'Well, let's get something tied around his head. Stop the bleedin'. Then we gotta figure out a way to get him down to camp.'

One of the men stood and walked to where Tom waited nervously. 'Easy, boy,' he crooned. 'We're gonna do what we can for 'im.'

He pulled Thad's bedroll from behind the saddle and cut a long strip from a blanket. Returning to the

168

prostrate figure he wrapped it tightly around his head.

'So how do we get 'im to camp?'

'We could walk back and get a wagon.'

'Take too long. Be dark way before we get back.'

'How about we bring our team up here with a couple of them logs we got cut hitched up. We could lash 'em together, put his blankets and stuff on 'em, then lay him on that. Let the team drag 'im to camp.'

'Be a pretty rough ride.'

'Better'n leavin' him here.'

'Can't think of a better idea.'

Half an hour saw Thad laid out as carefully as they could manage on the twin logs. They had even stripped the saddle blanket and pad from his horse, and put the saddle back on without them. Along with his bedroll, it made a decent pallet for the rough, bouncing trek to where the rest of the group labored. One led the team. One walked beside Thad, ready to catch him if he threatened to roll off the logs on the slopes. The third walked behind, leading Tom.

Two hours later the odd procession approached the busy encampment. A young boy burst from the collection of tents and ran to meet them. Five minutes later he raced back to the camp. He ran directly to where Corky and her parents were fitting logs onto the beginnings of a house.

'Hey, it's that gunfighter! Somebody done shot 'im!'

Coralee whirled, instantly forgetting the log she was holding in place. 'What gunfighter?' she demanded.

'That one what brung you back when you got debuted.'

A half-squeal of despair escaped her lips. 'Where is he?'

The lad pointed. 'Ed an' Ed an' Ted are bringin' him.'

Without waiting for any further information, Coralee grabbed at the sides of her long dress. She pulled the sides up to free her feet and ran as fast

170

as she could toward the approaching team of Belgian horses.

As she approached, she shouted to the Ed that was leading the team. 'Is he OK? Is he alive?'

Ed waited until she was close enough he didn't need to shout. 'He's alive, but I don't know for how long. Looks like he got it right between the eyes.'

That half-squeal of despair slipped through her lips again. She didn't slow her approach until she dropped on her knees onto the logs at Thad's head.

'Oh! Oh dear!' she said as she took in the blood-soaked strip of blanket around his head.

She laid her head on his chest. The rhythmic sound of his heart beating strongly sent a thrill of hope surging through her.

'Oh, hurry, Ted! Get him to my tent.'

She addressed the boy who had brought her the message. 'Eddie, go get a bucket of water and bring it to my tent.'

It seemed like it took forever for

them to get to the camp. By the time they had, nearly everyone in the group had assembled in a mixture of concern and curiosity.

As Coralee kept up a litany of unnecessary directions, the two Eds lifted Thad and carried him into her tent. They laid him, as directed, on the blankets that served as her bed.

Kneeling beside him, she swiftly removed the tightly wound blanket strip from his head. Using it as a rag, she dipped it in the bucket of water Eddie had brought. Carefully she began the work of cleansing the blood from his face and head, so she could assess the extent of damage.

Cora, her mother, knelt on the other side of Thad, helping, holding Thad's head still, catching the rivulets of bloody water that trickled onto his closed eyelids. As they worked, Coralee's attitude slowly began to change. Over her shoulder she addressed those she felt, rather than saw, standing behind her. 'I don't think the bullet went in. It looks like it hit his head and glanced up.'

'Really?' her father responded. 'He's too hard-headed for a bullet to get through?'

Coralee, for once, ignored her father's effort to draw her into a duel of witticisms. 'It plowed an awful furrow, though.'

'That's a scalp wound, though,' Cora observed. 'They bleed a lot, but they heal well, usually.'

'If it didn't hit hard enough to make his brain bleed inside,' Coralee worried.

'It's not bleeding much now.'

'Oh, Thad,' Coralee said, her voice pleading, revealing her feelings more fully than she meant to. 'You've got to be OK. You just have to.'

Cora looked over the top of Coralee's head at Walt. The look they exchanged revealed they both knew that hope was almost certainly futile.

16

Pain. Pain that assaulted deliberately and fiercely. A red sheen of pain that pounded against him. He willed it to go away. It pounded back in complete disregard, with every beat of his heart. It felt as if his heart itself were slamming a hammer into his forehead in rhythmic blows.

He moaned slightly.

From somewhere far distant, a voice responded instantly. 'Thad? Thad? Can you hear me?'

He should know that voice. Something in it drew him, pulled at him, made him want to respond. But the pain was a red blanket between him and the voice. He tried to respond, but nothing came out except another slight moan.

A cool hand cupped the side of his face. 'Thad? Thad, wake up. You need to wake up, Thad.'

He understood. He was trying. He really was trying. But it was like trying to climb up out of some thick darkness that clung to him, gripped him, held him down. The best he could do was make what noise he could from the darkness and the pain. He moaned again.

The voice was closer now. 'Come on, Thad. You can do it. You have to wake up, sweetheart. For me. Please? Please try, Thad. Try to open your eyes.'

Sweetheart? The voice called him 'sweetheart'. Did he have a sweetheart? He couldn't remember. It hurt too much. The darkness was too thick. Too heavy.

Moist lips touched his cheek. They moved to his mouth, touching his lips gently. The hand stroked the side of his face. Even through the pain, that felt good. 'Thad, it's me, sweetheart. It's Corky. Wake up, Thad.'

Corky. The name was familiar. It matched the voice, somehow, but he couldn't tell how or why. Her breath was sweet. He wanted to feel her lips again, but didn't know how to ask. He needed to look at her.

'Open your eyes, sweetheart. You can do it. Just concentrate. Just think about your eyes, and open them. Open your eyes, Thad.'

He thought about his eyes. He concentrated on trying to open them. He knew he should be able to do that. As he tried, he moved his head slightly. The movement sent new waves of pain shooting through his head. His eyes flew open.

'Oh!' Coralee squealed in delight. 'You did it! You opened your eyes! Oh, Thad!'

His eyes were open. He knew that because of the pain, as that light flooded in. He fought to focus them. Everything was a blur.

Slowly something began to take form in front of him. He frowned in concentration. The movement of his forehead as he frowned sent another wave of pain through him. Once again, the pain served as a clearing agent. His eyes began to focus.

Filling his clearing vision was the most beautiful vision he had ever seen. Blue eyes, brimming with moisture, looked back into his. Between them, a bridge of freckles arched across a dainty nose. Auburn hair framed a face more wonderful than any mountain vista his eyes had ever beheld.

'Corky,' he croaked.

She squealed in delight, throwing herself across him, her head on his chest. 'Oh, Thad! I knew you'd wake up. I just knew it.'

His arm felt as if it were made of lead as he lifted it to wrap it around her. She raised her head and looked into his eyes again. 'Does it hurt a lot?'

He licked his dry lips, working his mouth to try to create enough moisture in mouth and throat to be able to talk. 'Feels like a doozie of a hangover,' he croaked. 'What happened?'

'You got shot.'

'Shot?'

'Somebody shot you.'

'Who? Where?'

Memories came flooding back as he became more and more oriented.

'Long.' He answered his own question. 'He musta been layin' for me.'

He looked into her face, still inches from his own. A random thought crossed his mind that his breath must smell terrible to her. 'I guess I got careless,' he lamented. 'I knew this was the valley you were in. I was afraid he'd make another try at you. I couldn't let him get to you. I was hurryin' too much.'

'It's OK. He didn't kill you. Father says he must have been downhill from you. He hit you in the head, but it had angle enough it didn't penetrate. It made a pretty good furrow in your scalp, though.'

'Gave me a right good headache,' he responded, as words began to come more easily.

'Father says I should just forget

about you though.'

'Why's that?'

'He says anyone that's hard-headed enough to stop a bullet isn't someone I ought to be interested in.'

'Did you tell him he's too late?'

'What? Why?'

'You already called me 'sweetheart'. Remember?'

'When did I call you that?'

'When you was tryin' to get me to wake up.'

She opened her mouth to deny it, then to think of some witty comeback, then just said, 'You weren't supposed to be awake enough to remember that.'

'I remember what your lips felt like, too.'

He was glad his vision was returning to normal. Otherwise, he wouldn't have been able to see how furiously she blushed.

17

'Denver!'

'What?'

Thad stared into the face of Coralee's quizzical eyes. 'Denver. Just as sure as anything.'

'What is Denver?'

'That's a city.'

'I know that's a city!'

'Then why'd you ask?'

'To see if you had your head working enough that you'd know what it was.'

'So we agree.'

'About what?'

'That Denver's a city.'

'Well, I guess so.'

'OK. So that's settled at least.'

She smiled openly at him. 'You're getting better way too fast. I may have to scrub your head to get you back in line.'

'No thanks. It hurts enough already.'

She leaned over him and kissed his forehead lightly. 'There. That help?'

The arm that was still around her pulled her toward him. Their lips met, and neither seemed in any hurry for the contact to end.

She pulled back, but not very far. 'Now what made you think you could get away with that?'

Instead of answering, he asked, 'How long was I out?'

'All day yesterday, and today, up to now.'

'Two days. That's way too long.'

'So what's the deal with Denver?'

'That's where Long's headin'.'

She frowned, trying to figure out if he was serious or if he was taking a page from her book, making some long convoluted explanation that would end in nonsense. 'How do you know that?'

'It just came to me. He's got a pocketful of money. Everywhere he goes, more and more people know about him, or are chasin' him. If he goes to a city, he can get lost in the crowd. There'll be women there willin' to get smacked around if he spends enough on 'em. Or enough of 'em that he can stay on the move and keep findin' another one. He maybe ain't thought of goin' to Denver yet, but I'm bettin' he either has or he will.'

'So you won't be able to find him. That means you don't need to chase him any more.'

He shook his head in disagreement, then immediately regretted the action. He waited until the rush of pain subsided and the tent stopped spinning. 'That means I gotta get after him in a hurry, so I can catch up with him before he gets there.'

She stared at him in open-mouthed amazement. 'You are in no shape to be going anywhere! You were nearly killed! You've lost all kinds of blood.'

'I couldn't have.'

'What do you mean? You did.'

'I couldn't have lost all kinds of blood.'

'And just why do you think that?'

182

'As far as I know, I only have one kind.'

'Oh, so you think you're a thorough-bred, do you?'

'No, I think I'm more like a thoroughbled.'

She giggled instead of continuing the nonsense. 'Whatever you are, you are not riding off into the sunset after that monster.'

'Yeah, you're right about that.'

Her eyes lit up with excitement. 'So you're giving up the chase?'

'No. I'm waiting until morning, so I'm not riding into the sunset.'

She stood up and stamped her foot. 'You are in no shape to be riding! You have to have time to recover.'

'If I wait, he'll get away again. If he does, he'll be doin' what he's been doin' to more and more women. And he's started killin' in cold blood now, instead of just when he gets mad and goes nuts. That means as soon as he runs out of money, he'll kill someone else to rob 'em. I don't want all that on my conscience.'

'It won't be on your conscience! It's not you doing all those things.'

'No, it ain't me. But it's me that's accepted the job of stopping him. If I don't even try any more, then I'll be just as guilty as he is.'

She opened her mouth twice to form an argument that might dissuade him, then closed it again. 'I really, really don't want you to leave,' she said finally.

He looked into the twin pools of her impossibly blue eyes a long moment. He took a deep breath. 'I don't wanta leave, either. I want to just stay here with you more than I've ever wanted anything in my life. But I want you to be able to look at me without being ashamed.'

'I could never be ashamed of you.'

'You should be, if I back down on a promise when I don't have to.'

'I still wouldn't be.'

'Sooner or later you would. And I would. And I ain't gonna live the rest of my life bein' ashamed of who I am or what I did. Or didn't do.'

She tried in vain to think of an answer, but couldn't. She well understood the code of integrity that drove him. She understood it, shared it, knew it was good and right. It would be wrong for her to try to persuade the man she loved to break that code.

He saved her the trouble of trying to find an answer. 'If you'll steady me a bit, I'll see how much the world spins when I stand up.'

'Are you sure you want to try that yet?'

'No time like the present.'

He knew it was going to be difficult to stand. He knew the world would turn in vertigo-inducing spins if he managed to get to his feet. He also hoped Coralee would hang on to him real tight to keep him from falling.

He did. It did. She did not disappoint him.

It took a lot more tries than he expected before he could balance well enough to walk at all. When he finally felt able to walk out into the sunlight, he kept an arm around Coralee's shoulders. Sometimes he needed the balance and support. Sometimes he just needed to have his arm around her, to feel her arm protectively around his waist, to smell the freshness of her hair.

As sundown approached, the group gathered as they had in the wagon train, eating together, talking, sharing, singing. Little by little Thad's head cleared. He would be fine by morning. He'd get up at daybreak, and get back on Long's trail.

By the time Coralee had helped him back to her tent he was much less confident of his ability. Supper had tasted wonderful. He had eaten and drunk far too much for his shrunken stomach, but the fullness felt comfortable.

Inside the tent he eased down onto the bed. Only then did he realize her tent only had the one bed. She had been sleeping beside him since he had been carried in.

'Have you been here with me the whole time?' he marvelled.

'Of course. You don't think I'd let somebody else take care of you, do you?'

Lying down felt good. His head felt clearer. 'Didn't you leave something out of that statement?'

'What statement?'

'The one you just made.'

'I said, 'You don't think I'd let somebody else take care of you, do you?''

'Yeah. See?'

'See what?'

'You left somethin' out.'

'What did I leave out?'

'Wasn't you supposed to say somethin' like, 'You don't think I'd let somebody else take care of you, do you, sweetheart?''

She giggled, suddenly realizing what he was driving at. 'And what makes you think I might be inclined to say something like that?'

'We already talked about that. You said it when I was still asleep. But I ain't heard you say it since I woke up.'

'I haven't heard you call me that, either.'

187

'Yeah, but I'm a man.'

'What on earth does that have to do with anything?'

'Men don't say stuff like that.'

'Listen, Thadeus Palmer, if we're going to be married, you had darned well better learn how to say, 'sweetheart', and 'honey', and 'I love you', and 'you're beautiful', and a whole lot more things like that.'

'Wuoow! Wait a minute! Did you say married?'

'Do you think you're going to get by without marrying me, now? As you have already noticed, I've been sleeping right there beside you since Ed and Ed and Ted brought you here. Do you think my father will let you get away without marrying me, after you've been sleeping with me?'

He laughed hard enough the tent began to go in circles. When it steadied again, he said, 'Well, then, I suppose I should start practicing. Sweetheart. Honey. I love you. You're beautiful.'

She came into his arms, careful not

to jostle him too much. 'Oh, you learn fast. This is going to be fun! Sweetheart. Honey. I love you, too.'

She kissed him, then pulled away and drew back. She sat on the floor of the tent, staring at him in the dim lantern light.

A sudden thought intruded into the other wonderful things his mind was dwelling uncontrollably on. 'By the way, what's with the name 'Ed' in this outfit?'

She giggled. He loved the sound of that giggle! 'Well, there's Ed Hornesby and Ed Sensibaugh, that helped Ted bring you here. Then there's Ed Thurston and Ed Montgomery and little Eddie McCoy. For a while I thought the condition to be part of this community was to be named Ed. I thought the only reason they let Father be the leader is because his middle name is Edward.'

'Never saw so many Eds in one place in my life.'

'It does save a lot of trouble. When

someone yells, 'Ed! Supper's ready,' every man in the outfit quits work.'

'Easy to get acquainted, too. All I have to do is call every man I meet 'Ed', and chances are, I'll be right.'

He couldn't remember falling asleep. Some time during their conversation his exhaustion overcame him. When he wakened it was daylight. Just a few minutes, then he had to get up and start stirring about. He needed to get on Long's trail.

When next he woke, Coralee was kneeling beside him. 'You need to get up, sweetheart. It's almost time for supper.'

The sound of her calling him 'sweetheart' washed away his frustration at having slept the day away. Maybe one more day wouldn't make all that much difference.

18

His head still throbbed intolerably. From time to time, a wave of dizziness swept over him. Each time, he gripped the saddle horn and waited for it to pass. Each time it seemed to pass a little more quickly, though.

Little by little he schooled himself to move his head slowly. He learned to turn his whole body instead of twisting his neck. He learned half a dozen other little things to keep it from recurring so often.

By noon it was getting better. At a clear, swift-flowing stream, he dismounted for the first time. He felt slightly dizzy, but not nearly as bad as he had expected. He slipped the bit from his horse's mouth and refastened the bridle, with the bit beneath his chin. He let him drink, then move over to a patch of lush grass, where he began munching eagerly.

He knelt beside the stream and leaned over to get a drink. The dizziness swept over him as he lowered his head. He kept going forward, head first into the creek.

The icy water revived him instantly, clearing the sudden cobwebs from his head that had surprised him. He climbed slowly out onto the bank. He swiped the water from his face with his hand. He felt his jaw again, then moved his hand around over his jaw, his chin, his upper lip. 'Corky's been shavin' me, while I slept,' he marveled. 'I didn't even notice. Mighty smooth shave, too. Had to've been last night, and I still ain't got hardly any stubble.'

He wanted to wring the water from his dripping clothes, but wasn't sure he could undress and dress again without the dizziness overwhelming him. He settled for getting a cloth from his saddle-bag and cleaning his gun and holster carefully. 'I'll work some saddle soap into the holster later,' he muttered, 'so's it don't stick.'

He retrieved a packet wrapped in oil paper from the saddle-bag. Sitting down on a large rock, he opened it and began munching on the sandwich Coralee had packed for him. He knew there were several more in the saddle-bag.

As he put the soft rag he had used on his gun back in the pouch, he noticed another packet of some kind. He took it out, studying it with a puzzled look. Through the oil paper, it looked like a clump of hair. He unwrapped it carefully. As he did, he realized with a rush that it was Coralee's hair. 'She cut a hank o' hair for me to carry,' he marveled.

He closed his eyes and lifted it to his face. The scent of her hair brought her memory in a giant wave that swept over him, threatening his equilibrium more than the dizziness of his concussion.

He put it back in the oil paper reluctantly. He folded it back into a packet carefully, hoping he could seal in that scent so it wouldn't get lost. He put it in his shirt pocket, where he could retreat into its magic from time to time.

With a great effort he replaced Tom's bridle, climbed into the saddle, and continued on his way.

The second day was markedly better. He still had a headache, but he rode erect, bearing his weight in the stirrups instead of sitting flat in the saddle. He nudged Tom to a swift trot, and found that he tolerated the increased pace quite well.

He had seen no tracks he thought were Long's. That was just as well. He hoped the increasingly crazed madman would wander around for a few days at least, before he hit on the idea of going to Denver.

That night he rode into a town too small to even boast a sign announcing its name. At least it had a saloon with rooms where he could get a night's rest. He asked around, but nobody matching Long's description had been seen

194

around town. He was in the saddle again at dawn.

When he stopped to give Tom a rest, water, and a chance to graze awhile, he tried drawing his gun. He frowned in self-disapproval. He got a jar of saddle soap from his saddle-bag and worked on the holster for a while. Then he tried again, with a little better result. He still wasn't happy with the speed or feel of it.

Throughout the afternoon he continually practiced drawing his gun as he rode. When his arm tired, or dizziness threatened to return, he would rest. Then he would resume, with a dogged determination to work his way past the effects of the slamming blow of a bullet against his head. Even though it hadn't penetrated, it had struck with a terrific impact, and he felt every foot pound of that impact.

Well to the side of the road he spotted what appeared to be a homestead shack. He veered from the road. It wouldn't hurt to inquire whether the homesteader had seen anyone of Long's description passing by.

He was halfway to the house when he spotted the body lying in the yard. He reined in instantly. He studied the surrounding country carefully. Nothing moved.

Warily, he approached the yard. He dismounted, gripping the saddle horn for a moment to ensure he wasn't going to grow suddenly dizzy. When he didn't, he stepped over to the body. It was a young man, probably in his early twenties. He had been shot once in the chest. The blood around the wound was dried in the sun. He had been dead at least an hour. Maybe longer.

Drawing his gun, Thad walked cautiously toward the house. He stopped beside the door, listening intently. Tiny sounds he could not identify drifted past him, but nothing else.

Crouched low, he rushed through the door, stepped sideways, and placed his back against the wall. The dim interior of the small shack came swiftly into focus. He instantly wished it had not.

Sprawled across the one-room shack's only bed, a naked woman stared vacantly at the ceiling. A round hole in her forehead guaranteed the eyes would never look upon the body of her dead husband.

A small noise spun Thad around, gun in hand. Sudden vertigo overwhelmed him. He staggered sideways, falling on to the body of the dead woman.

He scrambled to his feet, fighting the dizziness, recoiling from the shame of his contact with the victim's naked body.

The noise came from a makeshift cradle in the far corner of the room. Moving across the room, he saw a several-month-old baby, looking back at him. It smiled, kicking its legs happily. A feeling such as he had never experienced crept over him. It kindled a deep, hard core of anger he knew would not subside until he had put an end to the madman's rampage, and to that man himself. The face of Vince Long, which he had glimpsed fleetingly only once, was burned into his mind so deeply he knew he would recognize him anywhere.

Pulling blankets from the bed, he covered the dead woman, then walked into the yard and covered her slain husband. Then he picked up the baby. He . . . or she . . . he couldn't tell, clearly needed a change of diaper. He had no slightest clue how to go about accomplishing that task.

He settled for wrapping it in a blanket that he hoped would keep everything confined, at least.

As an afterthought, he grabbed several diapers from a neat stack on the rough, obviously homemade dresser.

Returning to his horse, he struggled with how to mount and hold the baby and the diapers at the same time. Eventually he walked over to a buckboard sitting in the yard. He reached up and placed the baby on the seat.

He returned to Tom and mounted. He rode to the buckboard, then reached out and gathered in the baby and diapers, cradling it between himself and the saddle horn, holding it with one arm. The hand of that arm gripped the small bundle of diapers.

'Sure hope it ain't far to the next place,' he muttered.

As luck would have it, it was less than a mile. This homestead was nearer to the road. A woman was in the yard, hanging clothes on a rope strung between the corner of the house and the corner of the corral.

She turned and watched Thad's approach. When he drew close enough for her to be able to surmise what was in the odd bundle that he carried, she picked up her skirts and hurried toward him. She was a stout, red-faced woman, probably in her late thirties. 'Land o' mercy, what have you got there?' she demanded.

'Baby,' he said, his voice sounding strained and hesitant.

'Well, land sakes, I can see that. But where'd you get it?'

He handed the baby to her. She uncovered its face. Her eyes widened. She looked up at him as her face paled. 'Why, this is little Sadie McCracken! What on earth has happened?'

Without waiting for a reply she turned her head. In a voice that could have been heard halfway to Denver she called out, 'Alfreeed!'

Moments later a man appeared at the far end of the corral, a pitchfork in his hand. He spotted Thad. He leaned the pitchfork against the corral and walked swiftly toward them.

'What on earth happened?' the woman demanded again.

Thad took another deep breath. 'I . . . let's wait till your husband gets here. I ain't sure I can tell this more'n once.'

She studied him as if he were the cause of most of the world's ills for a moment, then her face softened. She nodded, lowered her head and began cooing at the baby. Sadie responded with a radiant smile, kicking her legs in delight.

'What's goin' on?' Alfred demanded as he approached. 'Whose is the baby.'

'It's little Sadie,' the woman responded.

'Sadie?' He fixed a hard look on Thad. 'How'd you come to have little Sadie?'

Thad took another deep breath. 'My name's Thad Palmer. I been on a man's trail quite a ways. Been gettin' close.'

'Is that what happened to your head?' Alfred demanded.

Thad nodded, instantly sorry for the lapse. He waited for the brief wave of dizziness to pass. 'He laid up and waited for me. Pertneart got me between the eyes. I guess I'm hard headed enough it just bounced off. Laid me out, though.'

'He shot you in the head and it bounced off?'

'The good Lord just didn't want you dyin' till you caught up with him, most likely,' the woman affirmed with conviction.

Thad grasped for control of the story so he could get it over with. 'I rode into the homestead back up the road a mile or so, to see if they'd seen 'im ride through here. I found a man dead in the yard.'

The woman gasped, clasping a hand to her mouth as she held the baby in the other arm.

Thad ignored her. 'I found his wife inside. She's dead too.'

Both stared at him in disbelief. It was the woman who recovered first. 'Had she been . . . violated?'

'I'm sure she had,' he said. 'She was . . . naked, sprawled on the bed. She'd been shot in the forehead.'

'Oh, Lord God have mercy!' the woman exclaimed. 'Lordy, Lordy, Lordy, what's this world coming to? Oh, poor little Sadie!'

Alfred looked searchingly at Thad. 'Where'd you find little Sadie?'

'She was in her cradle. She made a noise, or I might not've noticed her. I 'spect she'd just woke up or somethin'. She smells like she needs a change pretty bad, but I don't have no idea how to go about that. I just wrapped her up in that blanket. I covered up both o' the others with a blanket, to try to keep the buzzards and magpies and such away till someone can go give 'em a proper burial.'

'Land o' mercy,' Alfred said, his voice soft, sounding somehow distant.

'At least that animal didn't kill little Sadie too,' the woman said, snuggling the child close, rubbing her cheek gently against the baby's.

As if wakening from a nightmare and suddenly remembering his manners, Alfred said, 'Well, get down and come in. We'll try to figure out what to do next.'

Thad shook his head. 'Thanks, but I need to stay on his trail. I think I've figured out where he's heading. I've got a good chance to catch up with him. He can't be more than an hour or two ahead of me.'

Alfred nodded. 'Little more than an hour, I think. Leastways, if he was the rider that went by here. I didn't recognize him, but I didn't think none about it.'

Thad nodded. 'Thanks. I couldn't just leave the baby there. The only thing I could think of was to bring it to the next place I came to.'

'You done right,' Alfred agreed. 'We're much obliged.'

His wife spoke up again. 'When you find that monster, don't go just shooting him.'

'What?'

'Don't go just shooting him,' she repeated. Her voice shook with fury. 'Either give him the hanging he deserves, or make sure you kill him slow. Shoot him in the knees and let him twist in pain a while. Then shoot him right where it counts, and give him time to know what just got shot off. Then gut-shoot him and let him suffer a while afore you do him in. A man like that don't deserve to die quick'n easy.'

'I 'spect he'll get what's comin' to him,' Thad said. 'At least I sure aim to put a stop to him.'

Maybe the homesteader's wife was right, he thought as he rode away. Maybe that would be better justice, even, than the hanging Vince needed.

19

Thad dismounted, studying the tracks in the road. 'His horse has come up lame, sure's anything,' he informed his own horse.

Tom tossed his head in perfect understanding of his master's words. Or so it appeared.

Thad looked around carefully. He was a full day away from the macabre scene at the ill-fated homestead. The country was becoming more and more settled.

Even so, he was close enough behind the object of his quest to be able to pick out his tracks amongst the others on the well-used road.

He mounted up and followed that trail with growing anticipation. An hour later he spotted a ranch yard a quarter of a mile from the main road.

With a knot in his stomach that

boded an end to his search, he reined Tom that direction. At least this was a large enough spread for there to be a number of people about the yard and corrals. That would preclude Vince's ability to just ambush the rancher, steal a horse, and continue to run. He'd have to go through the formalities of dickering, make a swap, pay the boot, and act as if it were a normal situation.

He approached the yard cautiously. Even the dogs seemed conspicuously silent. He rode around the back side of the house, dismounted, and proceeded on foot.

From a corner of the porch he surveyed the rest of the yard.

Directly across the broad yard, the bunkhouse faced towards the house. To its left twenty yards or so, the corrals began. They extended in connected circles until they encountered a larger-than-normal horse barn. On the far side of the barn several stacks of hay provided a supply of feed for whatever animals might be confined.

An ingenious series of water troughs extended through all the corrals. They were supplied by a pump at the end of the one nearest to the bunkhouse. That trough was positioned outside the corrals, allowing access to it from the yard. Filling that water trough caused its overflow to run into a pipe that led to the next trough, inside the corral. It, in turn, overflowed to supply the next one in line. From the one pump, every corral's water trough could be kept filled. From that same pump, water for the bunkhouse and cookhouse could be drawn.

Two men stood by that first trough. One held the reins of a clearly spent horse. Thad recognized him instantly as Vince Long. Three dogs sat in rapt attention to the conversation, which explained why they had failed to herald his own arrival.

Moving on a line that would keep his approach hidden from either man, Thad approached quietly. He was half a dozen steps away when he stopped.

'That's a fine horse,' the rancher was

saying, indicating a gelding in the corral. 'He'll carry you to Denver in fine shape. I'd need at least fifteen dollars boot to swap for yours, though.'

'This horse is a bit tired, but he's every bit as good a horse.'

'Well, he may be, but he's obviously lame. That cuts his value considerable.'

Vince hesitated, clearly pondering whether he had dickered enough to allay suspicion. His need for haste convinced him he had. 'Well, I guess I ain't in too good a position to haggle,' he conceded. 'I guess you got yourself a deal. I got to get to Denver.'

'So you can kill some more women?' Thad asked softly.

Vince jumped as if he'd been shot. He whirled, his hand moving toward his gun. When he spotted Thad, his eyes grew big as saucers.

'You!' he sputtered. 'You . . . you're . . . you're dead!'

'Not as dead as you're gonna be when you dance on the end of a rope. Unbuckle your gunbelt and let it drop.'

'What's goin' on here?' the rancher demanded.

'My name's Thad Palmer,' Thad explained, never taking his eyes off of Vince. 'I've been tracking this cold-blooded coyote all the way from Lone Tree. I've followed a trail of murdered men, and raped and murdered women, every step of the way.'

'You're dead!' Vince breathed, clearly struggling to explain Thad's presence.

'You tried your best,' Thad agreed.

He addressed the rancher. 'He bushwhacked me a few days ago. I'm too hard-headed. The bullet slid along my skull instead o' blowin' my brains out like he thought it did.'

'You can't prove nothin',' Vince declared suddenly.

'I can prove it all,' Thad argued. 'You were seen leavin' the saloon just before that gambler got stabbed in the back and robbed. That little ol' girl you raped before that, you left without killin'. She can identify you. Then you killed that homesteader, then raped his wife, with him layin' dead not thirty feet away. Then you murdered her too, but you was seen ridin' off. You'll hang all right. Now unbuckle your gunbelt and throw up your hands.'

As Thad talked, the rancher edged away. His own hand, as if of its own volition, gripped the butt of his gun. Watching Vince, his eyes grew harder and harder. If Thad somehow failed to arrest Vince or kill him, he was positive the rancher would finish the job for him.

'Don't shoot me,' Vince pleaded. 'I'll unbuckle it.'

He reached toward his belt buckle, then his hand streaked to his gun instead.

Thad was more than ready for the maneuver. Before Vince's gun was half-way out of the holster his own forty-five roared. Vince grunted, knocked backward, fighting to keep his balance.

A second shot from Thad's forty-five drove him back against the corral fence. His own gun slipped from his fingers.

A third shot, deliberately placed,

from Thad's Colt blew away most of Vince's groin.

The fourth shot finished anything the previous round might have missed.

The fifth round tore through the man's vile mouth, blasting teeth and tissue through and out the back of his head, into the corral, where it would be trampled into the substance that most closely resembled the nature of the man it was extruded from.

The sixth pull of the trigger brought the hammer of Thad's Colt down on the empty chamber that always rode under the hammer.

He squeezed the trigger twice more as Long's lifeless corpse slid down the side of the corral. Long came to rest in a sitting position, his head lolled back against a rail of the corral. His hands lay on the ground just beside him, palms up, in a pose that was almost a carbon copy of a young whore's body in Lone Tree.

Because he hadn't seen that victim, the poetic irony was lost on Thad.

20

He had never spit on a grave before.

The hands on the Bar None had dug a grave in the little cemetery up the hill from the ranch house. There were maybe a half-dozen graves there ahead of his.

They didn't bother wrapping Vince's body in a blanket. They had emptied his pockets, removed his gun and holster, then carried him up the hill and dumped him unceremoniously in the hole. By the time the grave was dug, Thad had told them enough of his atrocities for the usual respect for the dead to be totally absent. He was buried as they might have buried a rabid dog, more to hide the stink of decomposition than out of any lingering regard.

His body had no sooner hit the bottom of the grave than shovels began throwing dirt in, as if hurriedly to get him out of everybody's sight.

When the grave was filled, everyone stood, as if not certain whether they should do anything further. It was then, following some impulse that he neither understood nor questioned, that Thad stepped forward and deliberately spit on the mound of fresh dirt. Then he turned and walked back toward the ranch yard.

As if it were some established ritual, every hand in attendance followed suit. If his victims were able to see, they would have approved. Perhaps they might even have rested in a slightly greater measure of peace.

Thad declined the offer of supper and a bed for the night. He was in far too much of a hurry to get back to a certain valley. What waited for him there, he was certain, would erase the memory of a lot of things no man should have had to witness.

It took him less than half the time to return than it had taken to cover that distance the first time. His mind raced with anticipation the whole way.

He was in no way disappointed.

We do hope that you have enjoyed reading this large print book.

Did you know that all of our titles are available for purchase?

We publish a wide range of high quality large print books including:
Romances, Mysteries, Classics
General Fiction
Non Fiction and Westerns

Special interest titles available in large print are:
The Little Oxford Dictionary
Music Book, Song Book
Hymn Book, Service Book

Also available from us courtesy of Oxford University Press:
Young Readers' Dictionary
(large print edition)
Young Readers' Thesaurus
(large print edition)

For further information or a free brochure, please contact us at:
Ulverscroft Large Print Books Ltd.,
The Green, Bradgate Road, Anstey,
Leicester, LE7 7FU, England.
Tel: (00 44) **0116 236 4325**
Fax: (00 44) **0116 234 0205**

BLIND JUSTICE AT WEDLOCK

Ross Morton

When Clint Brennan finds two men kidnapping his wife Belle, he's shot and left for dead. However, though he's been blinded, he realises his wife has gone. So, not giving way, Clint sets out after his wife's abductors, with his dog and astride his donkey. Belle, meanwhile, believes he's dead and when she's rescued by a rich man, she's told it's time to start again ... All this violence, betrayal and lies will end at Wedlock, amidst flames and bullets.

COLORADO CLEAN-UP

Corba Sunman

Provost Captain Slade Moran arrives from Fort Benson, Colorado, to investigate the disappearance of an army payroll and its military secret. A grim trail has taken him to the empty payroll coach and its murdered escort, with one soldier mysteriously missing. Moran is led to Moundville where he's confronted by desperate men plotting to steal a gold mine. Embroiled in double-cross and mayhem, Moran fears he will fail in his duty. Against all odds, can he succeed?

CANNON FOR HIRE

Doug Thorne

In the autumn of 1897, men flock to the wild Yukon Territory, searching for gold. But Tom Cannon, a one-time cavalry officer, has a different reason for making the hazardous trek north. Hired to find Emmet Lawrence — a greenhorn who'd disappeared seeking his fortune — Cannon searches the icy wastes and snow-capped mountains and draws a blank. No one remembers Lawrence, or knows his whereabouts. Then something happens that Cannon hasn't allowed for — Emmet Lawrence comes looking for him . . .